Catching Karma

A James McCarthy Adventure

By

Eldred Bird

Copyright © 2017 by R. Eldred Bird
All rights reserved. This book or any portion thereof may not be reproduced or used in any manner whatsoever without the express written permission of the author except for the use of brief quotations in a book review.

This is a work of fiction. Names, characters, places, and events are the product of the author's imagination or used fictitiously.

Any resemblance to persons, living or dead, is entirely coincidental.

Other books by Eldred Bird:

Killing Karma

info@eldredbird.com

TABLE OF CONTENTS

CHAPTER 1 7
CHAPTER 2 15
CHAPTER 3 21
CHAPTER 4 29
CHAPTER 5 36
CHAPTER 6 42
CHAPTER 7 47
CHAPTER 8 54
CHAPTER 9 61
CHAPTER 10 69
CHAPTER 11 75
CHAPTER 12 82
CHAPTER 13 89
CHAPTER 14 97
CHAPTER 15 103
CHAPTER 16 110
CHAPTER 17 116
CHAPTER 18 122
CHAPTER 19 130
CHAPTER 20 136
CHAPTER 21 143
CHAPTER 22 148
CHAPTER 23 154
CHAPTER 24 161
CHAPTER 25 168

CHAPTER 26 175
CHAPTER 27 182
CHAPTER 28 187
CHAPTER 29 193
CHAPTER 30 200
CHAPTER 31 205

For my father, Jack Bird, who bequeathed to me a love of old books and the knowledge that you never fail—you just learn how *not* to do something, and then try again.

Chapter 1

A warm, humid breeze drove ripples across the surface of the lake. The small waves split as they hit the bow of the boat and lapped at its sides. Two men sat quietly in their seats as a third yanked at his fishing pole.

Detective William Dugan did not look amused. "Quit moving that thing around and just let it lay there. The fish won't bite if you keep playing with it."

The young man continued his routine—jerk, reel up the slack, jerk, reel up the slack, cast and repeat. "It's a lure. The video on the company's website said you're supposed to pull it in short, quick motions like this to mimic the movement of a live minnow."

James McCarthy had never put a hook in the water before today, but he didn't let that stop him from sticking to his plan. Everything he knew about fishing came from books or the internet. In truth, almost everything he knew about *any* subject came to him through research, rather than actual experience. He made his living by gathering information from various sources, analyzing it, and then writing articles for magazines and websites. The subjects he covered could range from how to unclog a sink to navigating the Amazon River. Today, the subject was fishing.

"Just keep it up, Jimmy." Will reached into the cooler between his feet and grabbed a soda. "All you're doing is sending the fish over to my side of the boat."

James felt a little tug as the tip of his pole dipped slightly. He let some line play out and watched the tip again—another little tug. This time he grabbed the crank on the reel and jerked the pole upward, setting the hook. With a big grin on his face, he carefully worked the line, pulling in his first fish ever.

Donny Dugan grabbed the net and leaned over the side of the boat. He scooped James' fish from the water and held up the flopping, striped bass. The tall, red-bearded man grinned from ear to ear as he spoke with a slight Irish accent.

"Looks like a three pounder, maybe four," Donny said with a wink. "I guess Jimmy's eating fish tonight. All you're gonna be eating is them words, little brother!"

"Ok, so he caught *one*." Unlike his older sibling, Will spoke with no discernable accent. "Now let's just see how he does when he has to *clean* it!"

Donny unhooked the fish and dropped it in the live well of the boat. "How 'bout we make a little wager? Whoever catches the smallest fish cleans the whole lot."

"What if one of you guys doesn't catch one at all?" James questioned.

In the months since being unofficially adopted into the Dugan clan, James had learned a lot about his new brothers. He knew Will would be looking for a loophole if he came up empty. He would probably say something like, *if I don't have a fish, how can I have the smallest one?*

"Right, like that's gonna to happen." Will looked over at Donny. "Tell you what, if I don't beat this wet-behind-the-ears bookworm, I'll clean all the fish *and* I'll pay for the gas we burn today."

"You gotta top off my truck *and* my boat." Donny extended his rather large hand.

Will reached out, grabbed his brother's hand, and shook it. "Deal."

As they sealed the bet, the end of Donny's pole began to dance. The big man latched onto it and took up the fight. He let out some line and then slowly cranked the reel, taking up the slack as the fish moved around the boat.

"You know my truck has dual tanks, right?" Donny pulled the fish up to the side of the boat. James did the netting this time. "Well looky there, a nice, fat catfish! Wadda you think, Jimmy? Ten pounder maybe?"

"I'd say closer to fifteen." James hefted the catch onto the deck. "I think half the weight's in its head!"

"You and your damn stink-bait!" Will shook his head. "That's fine. I don't have to have the *biggest* one. I just have to beat that scrawny little baitfish Jimmy dragged up."

Donny baited his hook and cast it back into the water as James resumed his routine. The sun climbed higher in the sky above Lake Pleasant as the three men continued to talk trash and tell stories. The summer heat mixed with the humid tropical air moving up from Mexico, and caused large cumulus clouds to form all around them. August in the Arizona desert meant monsoon season. Powerful storms were known to pop up out of nowhere. Sitting at the foot of the Bradshaw mountains made the lake a prime target for the massive thunderheads. Donny kept a close eye on the dark clouds overhead.

"Looks like we got some big stuff building over us, boys. We better pack it in. There's been some nasty stuff kick up out here the last couple a days an' this little tub don't do too well in choppy water."

"Aw, come on," Will whined. "Head for a cove until it blows over. I just need one more hour."

Donny glared at Will as he and James both pulled in their lines and stowed their poles. Will knew that look all too well. His big brother was *not* going to budge. He finally gave in and put his gear away as well. Donny fired up the motor and headed out of the New

River arm of the lake, skirting the shoreline and hugging the canyon wall for protection from the increasing wind. As they emerged from the channel and into the rough open water, something caught Will's attention.

"Hold up, Bro!" He put a hand on Donny's shoulder and pointed to the south. "Looks like we've got a party barge over there trying to flag us down."

Donny swung the bow of the boat around and throttled back. Two young men in board shorts were jumping up and down, waving and yelling as they approached. Several bikini-clad young women were huddled in one corner of the pontoon craft. A couple more men were leaned over the railing on the far side. The taller of the two pointed down at some brush as he shouted toward Donny's approaching boat.

"Somebody needs to go call 9-1-1! We can't get a signal," he called out. "There's a *dead* guy in the water!"

Will reached into his pocket, pulled out his badge, and held it up. "Phoenix PD." He stepped onto the edge of a pontoon and launched himself over the rail, landing on the deck. "Have you guys touched anything?"

The young man screwed up his face. "Are you kidding, man? That's *gross*!"

Will stepped to the other side of the deck and looked over the rail. He could see the bloated remains of a rather large man laying face-up, tangled in the branches of a partially submerged tree. The body appeared severely mangled and scratched—little remained of his clothing.

Detective Dugan returned to the other side of the boat and addressed his brothers.

"Jimmy, grab my dry-bag out of the forward hold and get over here." He turned to Donny. "Get your ass down the lake until you can get a signal and call 9-1-1."

Donny nodded. "I'll wait for 'em so I can lead 'em in."

"Don't bother waiting," Will replied as James handed him the orange waterproof bag and made his way onto the pontoon boat. "Just tell them we're west of Barker Island on the south shore and get back up here. I might need your help if this storm decides to cut loose."

"Gotcha!" Donny eased the blue and silver bass boat away from the other craft, turned toward the open water, and gunned the throttle.

Will set his bag on one of the bench seats and opened it up. He pulled out a notebook with a pen attached, his cell phone, and a plastic zippered bag filled with blue nitrile gloves. The dry-bag also contained his gun. He pulled the weapon out and held it by the barrel as he pushed the grip toward James.

"Hold on to this for me," he dropped the gun in his brother's hands. "I might end up in the water, and I don't think I should leave this laying around."

James' eyes bugged out of his head as he looked at the heavy piece of blue steel in his hands. "What am I supposed to do with *this?*"

"Well first of all, I'd point it somewhere else." Will carefully pushed the barrel to one side. "Second, I'd make sure I didn't put my finger inside the trigger loop."

James quickly relocated his right index finger to the grip.

"Third, I'd probably just tuck it in the back of my pants so my hands are free."

The group of half-drunk, half-scared partiers looked on in disbelief as James fumbled with the handgun. After a couple of tries, he managed to get it tucked securely at the small of his back.

"All right." James looked lost and a little scared. "What now?"

"Now we gather as much information as we can and do our best to preserve the scene until the authorities get here." Will looked up at the building clouds as the wind tried to steal his cap. "They'd better hurry."

"What if we spread something over the branches, you know, maybe keep off some of the rain if it cuts loose." James turned to the young man who appeared to be the one in control of the boat. "Have you got some kind of a tarp or canvas?"

The man lifted the seat of one of the benches. "The boat cover is in the back of my truck, but I have a tent we set up on deck when we stay overnight."

James grabbed the tent and looked at Will. "I know he's been in the water, but maybe it'll still do *some* good."

Will nodded. "Not a bad idea, Jimmy. I'll take care of the body. You grab that pad and pen. I need you to get the names and contact information of everyone on this boat, and see if you can get a statement as long as you're at it."

"A statement?" James felt the barrel of the gun he had tucked in his belt slip lower into his shorts as he straightened his back. "I don't know anything about taking statements!"

"Just ask what happened and write down anything they say, word-for-word."

James picked up the pad and started taking down names as Will untied the tent and fought the wind to get the fabric spread out on the deck. With the edge of the tent gripped in one hand, the detective stepped over the railing, stood on the ledge, and leaned close to the dead man. He crouched down, trying to determine the best way to spread the cover over the branches without disturbing anything important. The new vantage point brought him face to face with the victim. Will stood straight up and yelled as he clung to the rail.

"Jimmy! Get over here!"

James dropped the pad and pen on a seat and ran to the side of the boat. When he got his first glimpse of the mangled body, he almost threw up. The only other dead body he had ever seen was his mother's lifeless shell. He had found her on the morning she passed quietly in their home almost a year ago. That scene had been peaceful, almost serene. This was quite the opposite.

"Look at this guy's face!"

James recoiled. "The whole side of his head is *missing!*"

"Screw the side of his head," Will snapped. "Get down here and look at his face!"

James held his breath and leaned over the handrail.

"Recognize him? I know he's a little bloated, but look close."

James swallowed the bile in his throat and took another look. He tried to imagine the face a little thinner and with more color. "He looks familiar. I may have seen him somewhere before." A face materialized in his memory as he studied the man's eyes. "Hey, wasn't he at the coffee house the night of that drug bust? This is one of Marco's guys!"

"Exactly!" Will spread the tent over the top of the branches. "This is Dino Romero. He's the reason I had to pull you in on that deal at the last minute. I'd busted him before, so I figured he might recognize me."

That cold January night at the coffee house in downtown Phoenix had been forever seared into James' brain. He remembered receiving the text from the man he now called his brother. The young writer had been called upon to pose as a heroin buyer in a police sting.

Will created the character of *Jimmy Ray* that night, and James played the role.

He had never been a part of anything like that before. The sting was successful in bringing down a major player in the Phoenix drug trade, but it also accomplished something else. After James managed to escape from the police, it made Jimmy Ray a wanted man and immediately earned him a reputation in the underworld of the major city.

"Do you think Marco had something to do with this?" James sounded a little worried. After all, the word on the street had Jimmy Ray responsible for the dealer's downfall. This thug was one of the people who had spread the word. "He could be coming after me next."

Will shook his head. "I doubt it. He's still sitting in the county lockup waiting for trial. He lost his power when word got out he was just Albert Bernstein, CPA . . . an Idaho pencil-pusher gone bad. No, I think people are still a little more afraid of Jimmy Ray than little old Al."

The sound of an approaching boat caught their attention. Donny slowed and then cut the motor as he tossed a line to one of the men on the pontoon. The young man tied the bass boat along side, as Donny climbed over the rail and onto the deck.

"County Sheriff's boat is on the way," he said as he peeked over the other side of the boat. "How bad?"

"Bad enough," Will replied before turning toward James. "Just to be safe, let's not mention Jimmy Ray when the County Mounties get here."

Chapter 2

The County Sherriff's skiff rocked from side to side as Will and James climbed aboard. Donny followed suit after moving his craft away from the pontoon and tying it along side the skiff.

"His name is Daniel Romero," Will cocked his head in the direction of the battered and twisted body next to the patrol boat. "They called him Dino on the street."

"And you are?"

Will held up his badge. "Detective William Dugan, Phoenix PD."

"Sergeant Mike Miller, Maricopa County Sheriff's Office." The deputy extended his hand. "How'd you ID the victim?"

"I busted him for assault once, and we took his boss down a few months ago."

"We?" The deputy eyed the other two men standing behind Will.

"Narcotics Division," he answered. "These are my brothers, Jimmy and Donny. We were trying to beat this storm back to the dock after fishing in the New River channel. These guys flagged us down when they couldn't get a cell signal."

"I got the witness' names and information." James handed the blue notebook to the sergeant and stepped back. "I took a few notes, too."

"I'm impressed." Miller fanned out several pages and studied them before turning back to Will. "He was pretty thorough. That, and the gun tucked in his back gave me the impression he might also be a cop."

"No, that's my gun." Will laughed as he watched James pull the firearm out of his pants. He held it with his thumb and index finger as he handed it back to its owner. Will tucked it in his belt and turned back toward the officer. "I didn't want to drop it in the water when I was over the side. As far as the notes go, he's just anal-retentive . . . and he's a writer, so he gets a little wordy sometimes."

"It looks like you asked all the right questions, Jimmy." Miller scanned at least a dozen more pages. "All of their contact info's here. I think we can let these kids go for now. You okay with that, Dugan?"

"We're outside the city limits, so it's your body and they're your witnesses," he replied with a grin. "I'm just here for the fish."

The sergeant motioned to a deputy on the pontoon craft. "You can turn these kids loose. We'll call for follow-up interviews if we need 'em."

Miller turned back toward Will. "This part of the lake *is* in Maricopa County, so I guess I'm stuck with this one."

James raised his hand like a timid child on his first day of school. "Um, can I ask a question?"

Miller held up the notebook. "Looks like you already asked just about everything, but go ahead."

Donny stifled a laugh. He stepped back against the boat's handrail and straightened his expression when Detective Miller shot him a hardened look.

"Take a look at him again." James pointed over the side of the patrol boat. "See how scraped up and twisted he is? I don't think he was killed here at the lake. It looks more like he was brought down by one of the recent storms. You know, tumbling down one of the washes in a flash flood or something."

"Yeah, that's possible." Will admitted. "What's your point?"

"Officer Miller, do you have a map?"

"It's Sergeant, but just call me Mike." He dug a map of the lake and the surrounding area out of a cubby under the bridge of the patrol boat and spread it out on the center console. James pointed to their position.

"Okay . . . um . . . Mike, we're right here. That means the body probably came down New River or one of these washes up here." He traced the path of a wash to the north with his finger. "If he came from anywhere up in this direction, that means he was killed in Yavapai County."

"Or at least dumped there," Will added.

Mike scratched his head and looked at Will. "Are you *sure* this guy's not a cop?"

James shook his head. "No, I'm just a writer."

"Let me guess, you write crime novels, right? Everybody that writes about murder thinks he can do my job."

"No, I write how-to articles and reviews. . . travel mostly," James replied. "I haven't published any fiction, but I do a lot of analysis before I write and I have to come to conclusions that make sense. What I'm saying here is . . . well, he's pretty broken up but there's no bruising around the wounds. Wouldn't that mean most of those injuries happened after he was already dead?"

Miller leaned over the side of the boat for a closer look. "That's the pathologist's call, but I see your point."

"And all of his blood seems to be pooled to one side . . . like he was lying in one place for awhile after he was killed." James pointed at the piles of sticks and trash floating in the murky water near the shoreline. "And look at all the other stuff around here. It looks like a lot of this washed down here when it rained up in the mountains the last couple of nights."

Miller nodded. "Keep going."

James studied the map again. "We didn't run into a lot of debris up the New River channel, but there was quite a bit in Humbug Bay when we came by there this morning. I'm thinking he came down one of the washes that empties into that area."

Will smiled at Sergeant Miller. "I hate to admit it, but I think he's right—he usually is. It's one of his most annoying traits. Looks like you can't avoid teaming up with Yavapai County on this one."

Miller didn't look amused. "Dammit! I hate this inter-agency crap. It always ends up getting messy. Everybody wants to take the credit, but nobody wants to do the work. And I hate to say it, but most of those guys up north are a bunch of small-minded cowboys."

"Total pains in the ass," Will agreed.

"So, you said you're narco and you busted this guy's boss? What's the vic's tie in? Distributor? Street level dealer?"

"He was hired muscle for a heroin dealer we took down earlier this year." Will didn't look at James. He didn't want to give away his brother's involvement. "He probably found another lowlife scumbag to work for. Listen, this guy had a partner he usually worked with—Bam-Bam, Boom-Boom . . . something like that. I can't remember the guy's real name right now, but I'll find it for you when I get back into town. Maybe you can get something useful out of him."

"I have a better idea." Sergeant Miller looked around and then locked eyes with Will. "I'm going to have to work with other agencies on this one anyway. How would you feel about getting pulled into the investigation?"

Will held up his hands. "Not my body. This one's on your turf, maybe Yavapai too, but nowhere near Phoenix. Hell, if he'd managed to drift a little farther south, he'd be Peoria PD's problem."

"But you've had a prior run-in with this guy and his death is probably tied to the drug trade in *your* jurisdiction. He might have been killed in town and then dumped up on the hill. I'd be willing to bet this is connected to one of the cases sitting on your desk right now."

"Okay, let's say I'm interested." Will checked out the map again. "How do we make it happen? I've got a full caseload right now, and I don't usually work homicides. My captain isn't likely to just let me run off chasing bodies in the desert, especially outside the city limits."

"You leave that to me." Miller had a crooked smile on his face. "You know the county sheriff. I'm sure he has some leverage he can use to get you reassigned. He's got leverage on *everybody*. Besides, if it *is* connected to one of your cases, you're already in up to your neck."

"Sounds like I'm on this whether I like it or not." Will reached for his wallet and pulled out a business card. "Give me a call when you get the official word. In the meantime, I'll see what I can dig up on my end."

Miller stuffed the card in his pocket as the brothers stepped over the side and boarded Donny's boat. He untied the line securing the two boats together and tossed it to Will, then looked at James.

"That was a good theory, kid." He motioned toward Will. "If you get anymore ideas, let your brother know. It might be interesting to see what else you come up with."

Will smirked. "Yeah, he comes up with a lot of interesting ideas."

Donny throttled the boat south toward the main launch ramp, bouncing off the building waves. As his brothers settled in for the rough ride, the summer rain began to fall.

"This is just great," Will shouted over the roar of the engine and the whistling of the wind whipping past. "It's not like I don't have a stack of cases piling up already. Carl is gonna be pissed if I get pulled away and leave him with that mess on my desk."

James shrugged. "Sorry, I guess I should have kept my mouth shut and minded my own business. I really thought I was helping."

"No, you made the right call back there. Miller would have figured it out eventually. You just got him there a little quicker. And once they pulled the RAP sheet on this guy, he probably would have sucked me in anyway."

"Well, if there's anything else I can do . . ."

Will cut him off. "Oh, there's going to be a *lot* you can do. I plan on keeping you in the loop on this one. And that loop will be a noose around your neck until we get this figured out. The whole flash flood thing is your theory, so you're helping me chase it down."

James looked a little worried. "What does that mean?"

"It means you'd better free up your calendar. As soon as I get the official word, the two of us are loading up and taking a little hike. We need to follow a few of those washes up the hill and figure out where our buddy Dino started his trip."

Chapter 3

A few seconds after the blinding flash of light, a loud clap of thunder rolled through Dugan's Public House in Central Phoenix. It shook the pictures and framed sports memorabilia lining the walls, but no one in the lively Irish bar seemed to notice. The usual crowd of rowdy patrons ignored the summer downpour. As long as the lightening didn't interrupt the power, they remained focused on the rugby match playing on the big screen in the corner.

The door to the pub slammed against the wall as two figures were shoved through the opening by a strong gust of wind. James struggled to get it closed and latched while Missy Franklin worked on getting her long, dark hair out of her face. The pair made their way to the bar and mounted their usual stools.

Donny handed each of them a clean bar towel. "You two look like a coupl'a drowned rats."

"Yeah, it hit pretty early today." James dried his face and then used a corner of the towel to get the water out of his ear. "The storms don't normally blow up until later in the afternoon. It's not even one o'clock yet."

"Well, I hope it blows itself out before we have to leave." Missy ran the towel over her wet, tangled hair. "You don't happen to keep a blow-dryer in this place, do you?"

Donny raised his hand and pointed over his shoulder with his thumb. "Jen keeps one stashed in the office. Might even be a little war paint in there too—you know, if you need to fix up your face."

She gritted her teeth. "Are you saying there's something wrong with my face?"

"Well . . . no . . . I just . . ."

Missy cracked a smile. "Relax, you big dork. I'm just messing with you." She slid off her stool and headed toward the kitchen door, calling back to her boyfriend as she went. "Don't get too comfortable, Jimmy. You've got a book signing in less than an hour."

No you don't. The voice of Josh McDaniel echoed in James' head. *I've got a book signing!*

Josh McDaniel was the name James used when he wrote. He had built a whole persona around his pen name. Imagining himself in Josh's shoes helped him construct more believable stories for his travel articles. Over time, Josh had evolved into a separate personality and became a fixture in James' brain. It was not unusual for the two of them to carry on conversations. These conversations often turned into full blown arguments. Whenever a public appearance was scheduled, Josh became quite full of himself.

Those people are paying to see me, you know.

James smiled to himself. "Good luck showing up without me."

He had a point. If James didn't show up at the outdoor expo, there would be no physical manifestation of Josh McDaniel. At the insistence of his agent, Simon Walker, James had been attending functions as the rugged, well traveled figure for several months now. Slipping into the skin of his alter ego was his least favorite thing to do.

"So, you're playing Josh today?" Donny chuckled. "You wanna single shot or a double?"

"Better make it a single. I don't want to give Josh too much freedom." James pointed at the lower cabinet behind the bar. "And stay out of Mom's stash. I could barely talk the last time she gave me that stuff."

Donny reached for a bottle of single malt Scotch and put a glass down in front of James. "I don't know how she drinks that stuff straight. Years 'a practice I guess. Will hits it every now 'n then too"

"What's Willy done now?" Margie Dugan walked up to James and pulled him off his stool, hugging him as tight as she could. "That boy got you mixed up in his shenanigans again?"

"Not yet," James replied with a smile. "But give him time. I'm sure he'll figure something out."

James returned to his stool and took a sip from his glass. The little Irish woman he now called his mother glided around the bar and grabbed a pitcher. She placed it under a tap and pulled the handle, speaking with a soft accent as it filled.

"Donny told me 'bout that mess out at the lake the other day. I feel fer that dear boy's mama . . . gettin' the call 'e's not comin' home." She placed the pitcher on a tray with four chilled mugs and hefted it into the air, balancing it above her shoulder on one hand. "It's just a cryin' shame."

Margie shook her head as she grabbed a bowl of mixed nuts with her free hand and marched off toward the group in front of the big screen TV.

"Did you tell her that *dear boy* worked for a drug dealer?" James took another sip of his whiskey.

"I might'a left that part out." Donny grinned and headed for a patron waving at him from the other end of the bar.

James took another sip and closed his eyes, letting the sounds of the pub fill his head. He listened to the rhythm of the music floating overhead and the buzzing of the conversations all around him. This was his ritual before making an appearance. It put him in the right headspace, as this was exactly the kind of place he imagined the rugged, well traveled Josh McDaniel would frequent.

Before entering Dugan's for the first time that chilly evening last January, James had never been in a bar before. Now this place was like a second home. Within its walls he not only found warmth, but comfort, acceptance, and a family—something he never had before. For the first thirty years, his life had been built around his mother, Rose. His father had passed before James' second birthday, so it had only been the two of them. She had raised him with a strict moral code, but in relative isolation. With her passing, everything he knew changed.

James smiled as he recalled Margie's words the day she learned he was now alone in the world. Her soft Irish accent made her voice sound lyrical. "Yer one a *my* boys now."

James felt Missy's hand touch his arm as her voice shook him out of his memory. "Looks like I'm driving today."

When his eyes popped open, they were greeted by the sight of his now properly coiffed girlfriend sitting by his side once more. Damp, tangled hair no longer covered her crystal blue eyes as she addressed him.

"Am I still talking to Jimmy, or is Josh already out of his cage?" She held out her open hand. "Whoever you are, give up the keys."

James fished through his pockets and produced the keys to Rose's old, white Buick. He dropped them in Missy's hand without arguing.

"I'm still Jimmy, but even after seven months I still can't get used to being called that. I was James for over thirty years, you know."

"If it still bugs you after a year we'll talk, but I refuse to call you James. It just sounds way too formal. Maybe we'll give Jim a try." Missy thought for a few seconds and then shook her head. "Nope, can't do it. You're stuck with Jimmy."

"That was a damn short year!" Donny laughed as he leaned against the back counter of the bar. "Get you something to drink?"

"Better make it coffee." Missy looked at the glass in front of James. "Looks like you've already got him loosened up for the show. Oh, and tell your wife thanks. I did end up getting into her makeup."

Donny picked up a heavy ceramic mug and headed for the coffee pot as James lifted his glass and took another sip. He put his arm around Missy, pulled her close, and whispered in her ear. "Thanks for watching out for me."

She smiled and kissed him on the cheek. "Yeah, you're still Jimmy."

"Yup, he's just plain old Jimmy." Will Dugan stood behind the pair as they spun their stools around to face him. "Who'd you expect? Wait, let me guess. New jeans, a camp shirt, boots, and you didn't shave this morning . . . you're playing Josh today."

"Nice job, Sherlock," Missy teased. "You should be a detective."

"I'm doing a book signing downtown." James slumped on his stool. "Simon is making me promote the *Camping Across the West* guide we published this spring."

"Camping?" Will let out a laugh. "*You . . . camping?* That's a good one!"

James frowned. "Not me, Josh."

Will planted himself on the empty stool next to Missy. "Well, you wrote that crap, not Josh. What the hell do you know about camping?"

"I've done my research." James straightened up and turned his stool around. "Have you even read any of my articles?"

"I don't need to." Will puffed up. "I've got *real* experience. I've done things you can't see on the internet."

"You've done things *nobody* wants to see on the internet," Missy exclaimed.

Will glared at her from under his overgrown eyebrows. "You think your boyfriend is so smart? I'll bet he wouldn't last two days alone in the wilderness before throwing in the towel."

Missy stuck out her hand. "I'll take that bet!"

"Wait a minute!" James grabbed her sleeve and pulled her arm back before Will could respond. "Don't I get a say in this?"

"Come on, Jimmy." Missy poked him with her elbow. "You know more than this baboon ever will. How many survival guides have you written? You could outlast him with nothing but the clothes on your back and a good knife."

"I wouldn't even need the knife!" Will barked.

"He's right," James interject. "The local native cultures carefully shaped different types of igneous and metamorphic rocks to form knives, arrowheads, and other tools. Obsidian and flint were the most common stones used in this area. "

Will lowered his head. "Great. Here comes the geology lesson."

"He just proved my point." Missy had a smug smile on her face. "He could win on brain power alone. You know he's smarter than you and that drives you nuts."

"Well, it looks like we might have a chance to find out." Will leaned forward so he could see past Missy. "I heard from Mike Miller. He got the coroner's report today. Our buddy Dino took a bullet to the head before he ended up in the lake. You were right about his injuries. Most of the damage was post-mortem, like he rolled down a hill."

"Or a wash," James pointed out.

"Yeah, or a wash . . . happy now?" Will sighed and continued. "Anyway, Miller got his wish. I'm on the case."

Missy threw up her hands. "I'm happy for you, but what does that have to do with camping?"

Will buried his head in his hands. "If you quit interrupting, I'll tell you. The first question I need to answer is where the body came from. That means I've gotta go back out to the lake and do some tracking. I need to figure out where he was killed."

"So, how do you plan on doing that?" James had a serious expression now. "Are you using tracking dogs or something?"

"Too much rain," Will responded. "They'd never pick up a scent."

"Helicopters?"

"Nope, just good old shoe leather. We need to be on the ground to look for signs."

"So you're organizing a search party."

"No, I'm thinking a party of two."

James nodded. "So, it's just you and your partner then."

"Carl?" Will grinned from ear to ear. "I trust that man with my life, but he can't make it up two flights of stairs without a break. There's no way he's carrying a pack and hiking up that mountain. Besides, we may have to camp out a couple nights before we find what we're looking for. Carl's not exactly what you'd call the outdoorsy type. His idea of roughing it is a hotel without room service."

"So who's going with you?" Missy was afraid she knew the answer before the question was out of her mouth.

Will looked past her and straight into his brother's eyes. "Don't plan anything for the next few days, Jimmy. You're about to get the chance to break in those new boots."

Chapter 4

James stretched and yawned as the summer sun peeked over the McDowell Mountains. Will sat behind the wheel of the red Jeep, guiding it off the freeway ramp and making the left turn onto Carefree Highway. He reached over and poked his brother in the ribs.

"I really thought I was gonna have to drag you out of bed this morning."

"I can't believe I let you talk me into this." James yawned again. "Couldn't you find some officer to go with you?"

Will shook his head. "Nope. Couldn't get the extra manpower approved until next week and it's supposed to be clear for the next day or two. I want to get back out there before another round of storms hit and wash away any more evidence. Besides, you're the one that came up with the theory about the body being carried down in a flash flood. I can't wait to see if you get anymore bright ideas once we're out there."

"I need to learn to keep my mouth shut," James grumbled.

"Too late, Bro." Will grinned at the sight of James' unhappy expression. "You stuck your foot in it, now it's time to back up your words."

"How long do you think this is going to take?"

"Depends on what we run into out there. If we find evidence he was shot or dumped close to the lake, we might make it home by dinnertime."

"And if we don't?" James really didn't want to know the answer.

"If it looks like he came from farther up the hill, we'll be looking at a couple of days. Hell, we could be out here for a week and not find a damn thing." The smile on Will's face grew wider. "It looks like you might get a chance to try out some of those survival skills you're always writing about."

"Great . . ." James frowned and pulled the bill of his hat down low over his eyes. "You're enjoying this a little too much."

"Hey, you're the one who's always talking about getting some experience under his belt," Will laughed. "I'm just doing what any good brother should—I'm helping you expand your horizons."

James pushed his hat back up and glared at Will. "By marching me up a mountain with a fifty pound pack on my back? Be honest, you're not looking for where that body came from, you're looking for some place to dump mine."

"Don't blame me for that thing." Will pointed a thumb over his shoulder toward the back seat. "You packed your own gear. I don't think mine weighs more than thirty. I'm sure you have a lot more crap in there than you're ever gonna use."

"How do you know what we're going to need?" James threw up his hands. "I'd rather have too much than not enough. You don't know how long we're going to be out in the middle of nowhere. Do you even know where we're going to start?"

Will shrugged his shoulders. "It's your theory, you tell me."

"It's *your* investigation!"

"No, technically it's Sergeant Miller's."

"Fine . . ."

James wiggled out of his shoulder belt and twisted his upper body. He reached into the back seat and pulled a stack of folded pages from one of the outer pockets on his pack. Slipping back under the seatbelt, he unfolded the papers revealing several topographical maps.

"You printed out maps?" Will pointed at the device suction cupped to the windshield. "That's what the GPS is for. I thought you were all up to date on the latest technology. Wait, maybe that was Josh. I get confused."

"A GPS is great," James replied as he ran a finger over one of the maps. "But what happens when the battery dies? I figured it would be good to have a backup. On a paper map we can also make notes and highlight the areas we've already covered."

"So you brought a highlighter too?"

"Three of them." He reached into one of the leg pockets on his new hiking pants and produced a small handful of writing instruments. "I figured we could use different colors to mark different details—yellow for our trail, green for possible evidence, and blue for other things we want to be able to locate again."

Will shook his head. "I don't know why Missy doesn't kill you in your sleep."

James ignored his brother's dig and went back to the map pages. "Based on the debris patterns in the water the day we were at the lake, my best guess is he came out of Humbug Bay."

"Yeah, we already know that. Anything else that might narrow the search area?"

James studied the map again. "Well, that guy was pretty big so it would have taken a lot of water to move him. There are some smaller washes that feed into the bay, but the biggest flow would have come from Humbug Creek. I guess that's probably the best place to start."

"I can buy that. We'll take a look around the area and figure out where to go from there."

The two brothers spent the rest of the ride in relative silence. Will piloted the red Jeep north on Castle Hot Springs Road until the pavement ended. They continued around the upper end of the lake, bouncing over the washboard road. James looked in wonder at the thick forest of majestic saguaros covering the rugged hills, their arms lifted in surrender to the building August heat. He had never seen such a breathtaking sight.

After a few miles, they turned off the main road onto an older track that looked like it was no longer being maintained. When they reached a flat area overlooking the rocky brush-filled creek bed, Will pulled off and brought the Jeep to a stop. He hopped out and walked around the front of vehicle, where he stood with his hands on his hips surveying the area below.

"Time to put your money where your mouth is, McCarthy."

James walked up next to his brother and looked at the wide floodplain. "This is crazy. How are we supposed to cover this whole area?"

"You're the analyst, Jimmy." Will put his hand on James' shoulder. "Figure out the best way to approach it."

"Maybe I can narrow the search area down a little." James looked around for a few seconds. "There's a lot of brush down there. If he was washed down any of these side areas, he would have been caught on something before he made it into the lake. I think we should start at the most open part of the wash." He pointed at a spot where the water had crossed the road. "That's the area with the least growth and probably had the highest flow rate."

"Sounds good to me." Will headed down the road.

James didn't move. "Wait, I don't even know what we're looking for."

"Anything that doesn't belong there," Will replied.

"How do we know what's evidence and what's just garbage?" James shrugged his shoulders. "Do we even know what he was wearing when he died?"

Will stopped and turned around. "You saw him in the water. Don't you remember what he had on?"

James shuddered. "All I remember is half his head was missing . . . and his eyes. I can't forget his eyes. You're the trained observer. Do you remember his clothes?"

"Okay, you got me there." Will walked back to the Jeep, rummaged through his pack, and returned with a file folder. He thumbed through the coroner's report and several pictures. He handed the photos to James and then skimmed the report.

"This says the floater had black jeans on. One shoe was still there . . . a black Nike, size ten."

"Can you please not call him the floater? It's disrespectful." James pointed at an image of the victim hung up in the brush. "Look at this picture. The neckband and one sleeve of his shirt are still there. It looks like a red t-shirt. There's some kind of picture or logo on it, but I can't make it out."

"Let me see if there's a picture of his clothes." Will spread the file out on the hood and rifled through more pages. "Nothing in here. I've got more on my tablet."

He pulled a small computer out of a case behind the driver's seat and booted it up. He touched a folder of image files and swiped through the thumbnails until he found what he was looking for. "Yeah, right here." He poked the screen and handed it to James.

"That's a little better." He zoomed in on the picture of what remained of the dead man's shirt laid out on a table. "At least with it out flat like this we can see more detail. It looks circular, but there's still not enough to make out the pattern. I guess we just have to check out everything we see that's red."

"Look on the bright side," Will smiled and kicked at the dirt as he packed the papers back in the folder. "At least he wasn't wearing brown or tan."

James grabbed a water bottle and looked at the rocks, brush and cactus covering the surrounding hills. "I guess we'd better get started. It's not going to get any cooler."

Will locked up the folder and tablet in the Jeep and the two men headed down the hill. When they reached the point where the main channel crossed the dirt road, Will stopped and looked in both directions.

"You take the wash north of the road and I'll take the south. If you see anything suspicious, don't touch it. We don't want to mess up any potential evidence." He pulled his phone out and checked to make sure they had a signal. "Text me a picture. If it looks promising, I'll come up and check it out."

The brothers headed off in opposite directions to begin their hunt. Will did as he had been trained and started walking the area in a tight grid, crisscrossing the floodplain as he worked his way toward the lake. The closer he got to the water, the more he found—paper, plastic bags, beer bottles, and several soiled diapers. He shook his head in disgust and continued his quest.

Having never participated in a search before, James devised his own method. He studied the main channel and came to the conclusion that he should concentrate most of his efforts in the highest flow areas. He paid extra attention to anywhere the water turned, thinking the centrifugal force might deposit objects at the outside of the curves.

He looked everywhere something could get caught, poking under bushes and inspecting behind rocks. Using a stick, he dug into the layers of damp sand

and gravel. He also found an abundance of garbage, but much less than his detective brother. The farther he got from the lake, the less trash he saw.

Hot and tired, James looked for a shady spot to escape the brutal summer sun. Finding nothing big enough to cast a decent shadow, he found a large rock in the middle of the creek bed and sat down for a short break. James took a few swallows from his water bottle and then pulled a white bandana from his pocket. He poured some of the water on it and rubbed it over his neck to cool off.

As he wiped the sweat from his brow, something a few feet away caught his eye. It wasn't the scrap of red cloth he had been looking for, but it was something that didn't belong there. He jumped up, grabbed his digging stick, and started carefully removing the sand until he was sure of what he had—it was an open wallet. He scraped a little more sand away to reveal an Arizona drivers license behind a plastic window in the center.

James grabbed his phone and fell to his knees, getting as close as he could to snap a picture. His heart raced as he fumbled to type a message to send along with the image.

JAMES: Main channel about 200 yards north of the road. Get up here quick!

WILL: On my way.

He sat back down on his rock and studied the picture. James couldn't believe his eyes as he zoomed in and read the name on the license out loud.

"Daniel Armando Romero!"

Chapter 5

The office in the back corner of the storage room of Dugan's was small, but the two women managed to work together in the limited space. Missy clicked away at the keyboard in front of her as Margie sorted through invoices and receipts on the other side of the old desk.

"Thanks fer helpin' me out, dear. Jen 'n Donny had an appointment this mornin'." Margie furrowed her brow. "I still can't get this whole computer thing figured out. Jen's been tryin' ta teach me, but I'm a little thick."

"It's not a problem. I'm happy to help out." Missy smiled and touched the woman's hand. "I know Jimmy's kinda dragging you into this century kicking and screaming, but he's just trying to help. Once we get all the old stuff entered and you learn the software, it'll make running this place a lot easier."

"Oh, I'm sure it will in time." Margie handed another pile of papers over to Missy. "Willy's been buggin' me ta do this fer a while now, but Jimmy's the first one ta convince me I should give it a shot. I trust that boy's got the smarts ta pull it off."

"Speaking of Will and Jimmy . . ." Missy stopped typing and took a breath. "I wonder how they're doing out there. They left pretty early this morning. Jimmy texted me when Will picked him up, but I haven't heard anything since."

Margie sighed and shook her head. "I'm worried 'bout those two. I don't know why Willy keeps feelin' the need ta drag poor Jimmy into his police business. I know Jimmy's smart 'n all, but 'e's no trained cop. That boy's had enough pain in 'is life. I don't wanna see 'im get hurt again."

"Jimmy can take care of himself," Missy reassured her. "As long as your number two son plays nice, I'm sure they'll be fine."

"The boy ain't been too good at that fer a while now." Margie stopped shuffling through the papers and put her hands in her lap. "Sad thing too, Willy was such a happy child. Sure, 'is brother had to stand up fer 'im when 'is mouth got 'im in trouble, but 'e never had a mean streak growin' up."

The old office chair creaked as Missy leaned back. "So what happened to him? What do you think changed him?"

"Well, the Army toughened 'im up, an' the police academy set 'im on a straight path." Margie paused and took a breath. "But 'is father gettin' killed in that robbery . . . well *that* made 'im mean. Swore that day 'e wouldn't rest 'til 'e tracked the bastard down 'n locked 'im up."

"That was almost five years ago . . . and he caught the guy, didn't he?"

Margie nodded. "Yup, 'e caught 'im alright. I'm bettin' 'e would'a beat 'im to death on the spot if Detective Stiverson didn't stop 'im."

"Carl?" Missy looked confused, "I thought they've only been partners for a couple of years."

Margie thought for a second. "Goin' on three years now, I think. Willy was still wearin' the blue back when he caught that fella. Every detective we talked to said findin' the man responsible in a city this size was damn near impossible, but Willy tracked 'im down."

Missy smiled. "That doesn't surprise me. When he really wants something, he doesn't let anything get in his way."

"No, 'e don't," Margie laughed. "I think that's what impressed Mr. Stiverson. The man took 'im under 'is wing 'n pushed 'im to move up the ranks. Once

Willy made detective, they partnered up. Those two been thick as thieves ever since."

"Kinda sounds like Carl took over as a father figure for him."

"Absolutely," Margie agreed. "I don't know what would'a happened, if 'e hadn't stepped in. Willy was a bit of a loose cannon after Michael passed. I know 'e was physically a man, but I don't think 'e was ready to be on 'is own yet."

"What about Donny?" Missy's voice got softer as she leaned forward. "I never hear him talk about what happened, but he seems to be ok now."

"Donny grieved, but bein' the oldest, 'e felt 'e had ta man-up 'n take responsibility fer this place." Margie took a deep breath before continuing. "Willy . . . well, Willy just got angry. I guess 'e used that anger to find the man that killed 'is papa, but once that was done, 'e wasn't ready ta turn loose 'n let go of it. Now 'e just turns it on anyone that gets in 'is way. When Willy goes off, Carl Stiverson is about the only one that can rein 'im in 'n get 'im movin' in the right direction again."

Missy lowered her head as she spoke. "I just wish he'd back off on Jimmy a little bit. He's been a part of the family long enough for Will to know he can trust him."

"Oh, I don't think trust is the issue anymore, dear." Margie smiled as she reached across the desk and squeezed Missy's hand. "I think Jimmy challenges 'im like nobody else. Willy likes ta think e's the smartest one in the room, but when Jimmy's around that ain't always true."

"Jimmy's book-smart, but Will's been around the block a few more times."

Margie cracked a little smile, "Willy might have more street smarts, but Jimmy knows a bit about everythin'. What 'e doesn't know, it don't take 'im long ta figure out."

"So, I guess the more experience Jimmy gets to go with his knowledge, the harder Will's going to push back." Missy shook her head. "That worries me."

"It worries me too, but I'm sure they'll find their own way eventually." Margie sighed. "'Til then all we can do is keep an eye on 'em an' make sure nobody gets hurt."

Missy leaned forward and planted her elbows on the desk. "That might be a little hard to do with them running around in those hills together unsupervised."

"Come on, Missy" Margie stood up and took her by the arm, pulling her out of her seat. "We need a break. The rest a this stuff can wait. Let's see what Miguel's got cookin'. Maybe we can sneak in a taste."

The women emerged from the back room just in time to see Donny come through the swinging door leading from the bar into the kitchen. He was grinning from ear to ear, his white teeth shining through his bushy red beard.

"Mornin' all!" His voice was more cheerful than normal. "What's for breakfast?"

"It's almost time to open for lunch, you big goofball." Missy reached up and tugged on his beard. "You're wound up today. What's got you so happy?"

Donny wrapped his arms around a surprised Missy and lifted her off the floor, giving her a tight squeeze before dropping her back on her feet. "Just having a great day darlin'!" Next he grabbed his mother and bent down, planting a kiss on the top of her head. "Beautiful day, ain't it?"

Margie put both hands on her son's stomach and pushed him away. "Lord above! What's got in ta ya this mornin'? Where's Jen?"

"She'll be along in a minute. Just finishing up a call with 'er mom." Donny turned and headed for the short, grey-haired man at the stove. "What cha got cooking, Miguel? I could eat a horse right now!"

"Sorry, no horse this morning." The little man grinned as he pulled a skillet off of a shelf. "How about chilaquiles instead?"

"Make it two." The tall blond woman pushing through the kitchen door had a smile almost as big as her husband's. Margie gave her daughter-in-law a quick squeeze before calling back over her shoulder.

"Just make enough fer everybody, Miguel."

Missy took her turn hugging Jen before opening the kitchen door and motioning toward the bar. "Looks like we have a regular party going on here. How about we move it to a table?"

"Good idea." Margie pushed her son through the doorway. "Donny, make us up a round a Bloody Marys."

"As you wish, Mother." Donny bowed with a flourish and then headed behind the bar.

Margie turned toward Jen with a confused look on her face. "Somethin' shake loose in that boy's head?"

"Yeah, he's acting kinda strange—even for him," Missy observed as the group sat down.

"He's just happy." Jen gave a coy smile. "We had a really good morning."

Missy threw her hands up and turned away in disgust. "TMI! I don't think his mother needs to hear this either!"

"No, not *that*!" Jen laughed, "Well . . . maybe a *little* of that."

Margie blushed, pushed her chair back, and stood up. "Maybe I should see if Miguel needs some help in the kitchen."

Jen put her hand on her mother-in-law's shoulder and sat her back down. "You can relax, Mom. We're not going to talk about that kind of stuff. Just wait for Donny. He can tell you why he's acting silly—well, sillier than usual."

"Here we go!" Donny circled the table, setting drinks in front of everyone. He placed an extra one for Miguel in front of an empty chair before taking a seat next to his wife.

Margie surveyed the table and picked up her drink. "Here, Jen, switch glasses with me. I think yer hubby shorted ya on the booze. That looks like it's all tomato juice!"

"This is fine." Jen pulled her glass closer, "I'm going virgin this morning."

"Virgin?" Missy giggled. "You can drink anybody here under the table, including me. Virgin is only for old church ladies and pregnant women."

Donny grinned even bigger than before. "Well, we didn't go see the priest this morning!"

Chapter 6

Will lifted his pack out of the Jeep and worked his arms through the straps.

"I don't know if you're really that good, or just damn lucky!" He holstered his gun and stuffed a few items in his pockets. "I guess it doesn't really matter. At least we know which way Dino came from now."

James adjusted the belt on his backpack. "I just tried to use logic to narrow my search area. I was really looking for a red scrap from his shirt or the missing shoe. I never even considered the possibility of finding his wallet."

"Must be all of that damned good karma you've got banked up." Will inspected the Jeep one more time to make sure they had everything they needed before locking it up. "Let's hope it holds out."

"Did you let Detective Miller know what we found?"

Will shook his head. "Not yet. All we've done is confirm he washed down from the hills like you thought. We still have to figure out were he came from. I'm sitting on this until we narrow the area down a little more."

"Are you sure that's a good idea?" James readjusted his heavy pack again, struggling to find his balance. "I mean, we found some new evidence—and he *is* in charge."

"I'm the ranking officer in the field, so it's my call," Will replied. "Hell, I'm the *only* officer in the field. Now let's get a move on before it gets any hotter."

Will took the lead as they started working their way back up the dry creek bed. When they reached the spot where the wallet had been, they stopped and studied the area. James pulled his maps out and looked them over again.

"I think we should keep moving up the main channel." He folded the maps and put them back in his pocket. "There are a few big washes north of here that feed into the creek. If we find any signs where they empty in, it might give us another direction to go."

"These mountains are a great place to dump a body if you don't want it to be found." Will pointed to the west as they walked. "I've done some four-wheeling up here before. Cow Creek Road runs parallel to this for quite a few miles. There's also a bunch of Jeep trails leading back to some old mining claims. They could have accessed Humbug Creek from any of those."

"According to the map, there are some roads to the east as well." James continued to scan the ground as they slowly made their way uphill. "I saw a couple of springs marked up that way too. If we're going to be out here for more than a day or two, we need to know where the water sources are."

Will scanned the cloud strewn summer sky. "If the weather-heads are wrong about the forecast, water may not be a problem."

"True, but we'll need a way to collect it," James pointed out. "I have some plastic bags. We can use the rain-fly from my tent to catch the water and funnel it into one."

"Are you for real?" Will shook his head and sighed. "That was sarcasm, Jimmy. You might want to look up the definition."

James gave him a dirty look. "I'm serious. Dehydration will kill you faster than just about anything else out here."

Will grinned. "Except maybe the snakes."

James stopped in his tracks. "This is all a big joke to you, isn't it? Do you know about the Rule of Threes?"

"Yeah, I did survival training in the military," Will shot back as he stopped walking. "In most conditions you can survive three hours without shelter, three days without water, and three weeks without food."

"In *most* conditions," James stressed. "Arizona in the summer *isn't* most conditions. We need to have a plan if we run out of water."

Will held up his cell phone. "Here's my plan."

"Right . . ." James turned and started walking again. "Until we can't get a signal or the battery goes dead."

Will put his phone back in his pocket. "You let me worry about that."

The pair kept moving north up Humbug Creek, scanning the ground and brush as they walked. The heat continued to build as the sun approached its apex in the summer sky. James pulled his bandana out and wiped his face. The humidity was high enough that his sweat was rolling off before it had a chance to evaporate. Getting cool seemed impossible. When they reached an area with a few small trees, James couldn't stand it anymore.

"Can we sit down for a minute?" He pointed out the thin canopy of a twisted mesquite tree clinging to the rocks on the eastern edge of the creek bed. "I need to cool off and who knows when we might find shade again."

"Yeah, I could use a break, and you've lasted longer than I thought you would." Will slipped his pack off and sat down on one of the roots wrapped around a small boulder. "Might be a good time for some lunch, too."

James removed his pack as well and settled into the cool, damp sand in a spot where the sun hadn't warmed it yet. He took a drink of water before pulling out an apple and a banana. He also unpacked a peanut butter and jelly sandwich and removed it from its plastic zippered bag.

"A peanut butter sandwich and a banana?" Will snickered as he chewed on a hard piece of beef jerky. "Are you stuck in the third grade or something?"

"What's wrong with peanut butter?" James held up the sandwich. "This is more nutritionally complete than what you're eating. It has protein for muscle recovery, carbohydrates for energy, and salt to replace what we're losing in this heat . . . all without requiring refrigeration. The banana contains more carbohydrates and potassium. When you're sweating this much, electrolyte replacement is very important."

Will got a smug look on his face. "And just how much extra water is it gonna take to wash that sticky mess down?"

"That's what this is for." James held up the other piece of fruit. "Eating a juicy apple after everything else cleans out your mouth. It's like nature's toothbrush!"

"Good. That leaves more water for me," Will quipped as he closed the bag of jerky. "All the salt in this stuff is making me thirsty."

James reached in his pack and fished out another apple. He smiled and tossed it to the detective. Will caught the apple with one hand and bit it without saying a word. After a few more bites, he hung his head and gave his brother a sideways look. "Ok, I'll give you this one."

Will finished his apple and threw the core into the bushes before leaning back against the boulder. He extended his legs and pulled his hat down over his eyes. "Siesta time!"

James finished his lunch and sat cross legged in the sand, studying the maps. He used one of the highlighters to mark a few items and made some notes in the margin. After folding the papers up and returning them to his pocket, he laid back in the sand with his head on his pack and tried to get some rest as well.

Hiking in the summer sun had drained James' energy, but he still was unable to sleep. Try as he might, he couldn't get comfortable in the creek bed. As he adjusted his position on the ground he could feel every stick and pebble. He shifted one way and then the other, finally rolling onto his side. Something under the sand poked him just below his ribcage. He sat up and pushed the sand away from the area expecting to find another sharp rock, but what he saw startled him.

"Oh my *God!*" James jumped to his feet.

"What the hell?" Will sprang up and instinctively pulled his gun, pointing it at the ground in front of James. "*Snake?*"

"No, look!" He pointed at a sun bleached piece of bone, studded with teeth, sticking out of the sand. "It's a jaw . . . a human jaw!"

Will relaxed his stance and holstered his gun. "You scared the shit out of me, Jimmy. Dino may have been missing a chunk of his skull, he still had his jaw. That's probably from some dead animal."

"Really?" James kicked some of the sand away from the broken mandible with the toe of his boot. "How many wild animals have you seen that have fillings and a gold crown?"

Chapter 7

The afternoon sun baked the desert foothills of the Bradshaw Mountains as Will and James continued picking through the dry creek bed.

"I found another one!" James pointed to what appeared to be a human femur sticking out of a pile of gravel built up behind a rock.

"Just take a picture and mark it on your map," Will called back. "I've got a couple more hits over here, too. This is starting to add up. We've gotta have at least two or three bodies here. From the looks of things they've been here a while. I think we found somebody's dumping ground."

James inspected the bone a little closer. "There's still some tendons and dried up tissue on this one, and it's not sun-bleached at all. I think it was probably buried. Maybe the rain washed out some kind of mass grave or something."

Will made his way over to the find. "Yeah, I think it's time to give Miller a call. We need a forensic team up here."

"How do you plan to call him?" James pulled out his phone and pointed at the screen. "We don't have any service. Are we hiking back down until we get a good signal?"

Will smiled as he slipped his pack off and opened one of the side pockets. He pulled out what looked like an old brick-shaped cell phone.

"Satellite phone!" He turned it on and unfolded the antenna. "I thought it might come in handy so I signed one out yesterday. You keep combing the area while I call this in."

James went back to his search while Will climbed out of the wash to get a better signal. Ten minutes later he returned and stowed the phone back in its pocket.

"Alright, since this stuff isn't from our homicide Mike's turning the scene over to somebody from Yavapai." Will picked up his pack and slung it over one shoulder. "I gave him the GPS coordinates, but I doubt they'll be able get anybody out here until sometime tomorrow morning. We still have a couple more hours of daylight, but I think we ought to go ahead and set up camp here for the night."

"Don't you think we should find someplace on higher ground?" James looked around the creek bed. "The sand might be a little softer to sleep on but if it rains tonight, we could get caught in the runoff."

"The forecast says that's not gonna happen, but Lord knows they've been wrong before." Will pointed up the steep bank he had just come down. "I saw a flat spot up on top. We might have to kick a few dozen rocks out of the way to get comfortable, but it should work."

Will led the way as they climbed out of the ravine. He stopped at a clear area between the brush and cactus covering the hillside and dropped his gear. James followed suit and the two set about the task of clearing the rocks and sticks littering the ground. Will formed some of the larger stones into a circle in the center of the clearing.

"Why do we need a fire?" James asked as he began unpacking. "We'll be lucky if it drops into the low eighties tonight."

"A few reasons," Will replied. "If it does rain, we'll need it to dry stuff out. It'll be a lot harder to light one after things get wet. We can also use it for light and to cook dinner."

James pulled a small bag out of his pack and held it up. "I have an alcohol burner for cooking."

"One more thing you didn't need to bring," Will prodded. "You could have saved close to a pound right there."

"You're right." James repacked the stove and stood up. "We could just cook over a fire. I'll see if I can find some wood."

"Grab some dry weeds too. We can use them to get it going."

"Can't we just use the alcohol for the stove to get the wood started?"

"I have a much better idea." Will grinned as he pulled a book out of his pack. James recognized the cover immediately. "I figured you could show me how to do some of the stuff you wrote in here—like how to make a fire without matches or a lighter."

James shook his head in disgust. "So bringing a pack stove was unnecessary weight, but hauling that book all the way up here for a stupid joke wasn't? I hope it was worth it."

"Oh, it's totally gonna be worth it." Will smiled as he thumbed through the pages. "I think I'm gonna get a *lot* of use out of this thing!"

"So you don't think I can start a fire without matches?"

"Or a lighter," Will shot back. "Not a chance in hell."

James crossed his arms and stood tall. "Care to make a bet?"

Josh invaded his brain.

What are you doing?

Will tossed the book aside and stood up. He crossed his arms as well, mocking James' body language. "I'm all over that. What are the stakes?"

Shut the hell up, you idiot!

James thought for a second, and then smiled. "If I can do it, you have to carry the heavier pack."

"Let's go one better." Will got right up in his brother's face. "Loser has to carry *both* packs!"

Don't do it!

"It's a bet!" James put out his hand without hesitation and they shook to seal the wager.

"I can't wait to see this," Will snickered as he went back to stacking rocks and clearing the ground.

Josh gave a parting shot as he faded back into the depths of James' mind.

Dumbass . . .

Eager to prove his brother wrong, James set about gathering the resources needed to accomplish his task. The desert landscape yielded more burnable materials than he expected. He was able to find a substantial pile of dried mesquite roots and dead branches. The spring grasses had baked under the summer sun to the point they would burn almost as quickly as the alcohol for the camp stove. He pulled several hands-full and added them to his growing pile.

He found a scrubby looking juniper tree clinging to the base of a rock face. Pulling a multi-tool from the pouch on his belt, he unfolded the knife blade and shaved some of the hairy bark from its trunk to help build a tinder bundle. He then extended the saw blade and used it to cut off a slightly curved green branch about two feet long.

Next he found a Spanish sword plant, a large member of the yucca family. He cut several of the long, pointed leaves and split them open, stripping as many of the tough fibers out as he could. He also pulled a dried rib from the skeleton of a dead saguaro before returning to the campsite.

Will looked on in amusement as James planted himself crossed legged on the ground and quietly went to work. He stripped the green branch clean and set it aside. Next he took several of the cactus fibers and braided them together. After completing three long braids, he worked them together to form a thick cord about three feet long.

Will couldn't take the silence anymore and finally spoke up. "What the hell are you doing, trying to macramé yourself a hammock?"

"I'm making a fire bow," James replied without looking up. "This is the string for it."

Will chuckled. "Idiot, you could've saved twenty minutes and just used your bootlace."

"If my bootlaces were cotton I could have used them, but these are nylon." He pointed at Will's pack. "If you actually *read* that book you'd know that a nylon lace can melt due to friction."

Will's amusement faded. "I would have figured it out without reading your damn book."

"So you prefer to learn by your own mistakes?" James was the one smiling now. "I'm perfectly happy to learn from other people's experience."

"Because you don't have any of your own," Will scoffed.

James ignored Will's dig and went back to work. He cut off a piece of the saguaro rib and shaped it into a spindle, sharpening both ends to a forty-five degree angle. He took another piece of the rib and carved a funnel shaped hole near one edge, cutting a 'V' shaped notch toward the center all the way through to the bottom. Finally, he carved another chunk of the rib into a hand-block to hold the top of the spindle.

As much as he tried not to look interested, Will couldn't help himself. He stopped unpacking his gear and watched as James prepared a tinder bundle and set it aside. He placed the remaining weeds and bark in the center of the fire ring and tented some smaller branches over the pile. He twisted the spindle into the string of the bow. Crouching with one foot on the notched stick, he placed one end of the spindle in the hole and pressed down on it with the hand-block.

"Here's goes nothing," James began to slowly stroke the bow, causing the spindle to rotate in its socket.

Will looked confident. "Nothing is exactly what I'm expecting. You're not even moving that thing fast enough to get any smoke out of it."

"I'm not trying to make it smoke yet," he replied. "I'm building up some wood dust in the notch. You need that first before you can create an ember."

After a couple of minutes James lifted the spindle and inspected the hole. "That looks like enough dust. I should be able to get something out of it now."

Putting less pressure down on the spindle this time, he began to move the bow back and forth, picking up speed as he went. About a minute later a small stream of smoke rose from the notch. James picked up the pace as the smoke began to build. When he was satisfied he had an ember he dropped the bow and spindle, grabbed the stick, and tapped the smoking dust into the tinder. He cupped the bundle in his hands and started to gently blow. The ember blinked and died.

Will jumped up and pointed at the cold bundle in James' hands. "I *told* you, you couldn't do it!"

"I'm not done yet," James said confidently. "I didn't think I'd even get *that* far on the first try. I'm just happy the string I made didn't break."

"How many tries do you think it'll hold up for?" Will looked to the west and smiled. "We need that fire before we lose daylight. If I don't see a flame by sunset, the lighter is coming out of my pocket and you lose the bet."

James held his hand up at arms length facing the horizon and closed one eye, focusing on his extended fingers. "The sun is a little over two fingers widths above the horizon. That means it should go down in about thirty minutes. We should have good light for at least another twenty after that. I think I'll have enough time."

Will had a confident smile as he watched James put his head down and reset the spindle and bow, repeating the same process as before. This time he didn't stop until the smoke was so thick he couldn't see the stick under his foot. Just like before, he tapped the smoldering ember into the tinder bundle and gently blew several times.

A small flame jumped to life. James continued to nurse it as he turned and leaned over into the ring of rocks. He placed the bundle under the edge of the dried grass in the middle of the sticks. As the grass caught fire he blew harder to spread the flame. In less than a minute the pyramid was fully engulfed. He added several larger pieces of wood and stood back to admire his accomplishment.

James smiled from ear to ear. "That was fun!"

"Son of a . . ." Will couldn't even get the whole sentence out without biting his lip.

Way to go, Jimmy!

Josh was bouncing off the walls of James' brain.

I never had any doubt!

Chapter 8

The first rays of sunlight cleared the ridge as Will rolled over for what must have been the twentieth time. Try as he might, he couldn't get comfortable on the hard, uneven ground. When he finally gave up and opened his eyes, he was greeted by the sight of his brother crouching by the fire.

"Good morning!" James smiled and held up a red plastic mug. "Coffee?"

Will crawled out of his sleeping bag and made his way to the fire. "Why the hell are you so cheerful this morning? I didn't sleep worth a crap. It felt like I was lying on a pile of rocks."

"Maybe that's because you were." James handed him the mug and filled another one with hot water from the pot sitting on a flat rock close to the fire, then dumped a packet of instant coffee in. "I slept fine . . . more than fine, in fact. I've never camped out before. The sunrise was amazing!"

Will took a sip from his cup and then stretched. "Your back doesn't hurt?"

"Nope." James pointed at the open flap of his tent. "I brought an inflatable sleeping pad. Between that and the extra grass I layered under the floor, I was pretty comfortable."

"Couldn't take sleeping on the pea, Princess?" Will shook his head. "I still don't know why you bothered hauling that tent up here. It's not like it's cold this time of year, even at night."

"I didn't want anything crawling into bed with me." James poured more water from the pot into a paper cup with instant oatmeal in it. "The three hour rule includes exposure to animals and bugs too, not just the elements. I also figured it would be easier to stay dry if it rained overnight."

"Did you rub your damn sticks together again to start that fire," Will sniped, "or did you use a lighter this time?"

"I put a thick piece of mesquite on before I went to sleep last night so there would still be hot coals this morning." James smiled as he poked at the fire with a stick. "All I had to do was put some more grass and sticks in there and blow on it to get it going again."

"You could have used a few pages out of that stupid book," Will grumbled as he sat down on a rock near the fire. "Got any more oatmeal? That MRE I ate last night is still sitting in my stomach like a rock."

James retrieved a packet from his supply bag and handed it over along with another paper cup and a plastic spoon. Will looked confused as he held up the cup.

"Why aren't we using the bowls from the mess kits? All you're doing with this crap is making more trash for us to pack out."

"We haven't found a source for water yet, so I'm trying to conserve. If we use the mess kits, we have to wash them." James held up a gallon sized plastic zipper bag. "We can just crush the paper cups down and seal them in here with our other trash."

"What about the plastic coffee cups? How do you plan to wash those?" Will looked confident that he had him in a corner this time.

James had an answer ready. "We can just rinse them out and drink the water instead of dumping it."

Will sighed and didn't say another word. He sat quietly watching the fire die as he sipped his coffee and ate breakfast. James brushed his teeth and freshened up with a couple of wet-wipes before putting on a clean shirt. After Will finished his coffee, they went about the business of breaking down camp and repacking their gear. As James tightened the final strap securing the top flap of his pack, something caught his eye.

"Hey, Will!" James pointed to the west. "Someone's coming."

Will jumped and spun 180 degrees as his hand landed on the gun strapped to his belt. He relaxed his stance immediately when he saw the sun glint off the gold star pinned to the man's chest. The officer's brown and tan uniform blended into the landscape. Had it not been for the movement of his steady gait, James might never have seen him until he was right on top of them.

The stocky Native American man spoke in a slow monotone. " Detective Dugan?" He extended his hand. "Nestor Yazzi, Yavapai County Sheriff's Office."

"Call me Will." He shook his hand and pointed to James. "This is Jimmy McCarthy."

Nestor turned toward James and looked him over. "You're not a cop." It was clearly a statement, not a question.

"No," James answered. "I'm just family."

"You don't look like family." Nestor's tone and expression didn't change as he spoke. "You married in?"

"I was kind of adopted," James responded. "Unofficially. . ."

"Stray dog." Nester nodded.

"Um . . ." James looked surprised. "I'm a stray dog?"

Nestor put a hand on James' shoulder. "Don't worry, I like stray dogs."

James wasn't sure how to respond. Something told him it was best not to until he learned more about the stone-faced lawman. As the deputy surveyed the campsite, his eyes settled on an object near the circle of rocks.

"Nice fire bow." He poked it with the toe of his boot. "Somebody forget the matches?"

James spoke up. "Will bet me I couldn't start a fire without using a lighter."

Nestor picked up the spindle and notched stick. He inspected it from every angle, even passing it under his nose before addressing Will.

"You lost."

"He just got lucky. Anyway, it's useless knowledge." Will pulled a lighter from his pocket and held it up. "One of these or a book of matches works a whole lot better."

"Until that thing runs out of fuel or your matches get wet," Nestor replied straight faced. "There is no useless knowledge."

"Yazzi . . . Navajo right?" Will bent over and picked up the bow. "I'll bet your father taught you how to make a fire with one of these."

"You need to stop making bets. You're no good at it." Nestor still didn't change the tone or cadence of his speech. "My father was a plumber. He taught me how to fix a toilet."

Nestor reached out and took the bow from Will, handing it to James along with the spindle and stick. He finally cracked his stone face and managed a little smile.

"Good job, Stray Dog. I like you." Turning toward Will, he straightened his expression once more. "You don't impress me."

"You don't even know me," Will protested.

"I know what I see." Nestor looked around the site again. "How's your back this morning?" He pointed at the outline of James' tent on the ground. "There was room for two in that tent, but you slept outside on the ground."

"How do you know I wasn't the one in the tent?" Will sneered.

"Because you're pigheaded, and your boot prints are all around those rocks." He turned and pointed at the layer of grass within the outline of where the tent had been set up. "Stray Dog is smart. He came prepared and also knows how to use what nature provides."

"Puppy Dog's never even been camping before, he just writes about it. He's got no real experience," Will growled. "You don't look all that prepared either. Where's your food and water? And your gear?"

"About 300 yards west of here," Nestor replied without missing a beat. "In my truck."

James pulled his maps out and inspected one of the pages before showing it to Deputy Yazzi. "We parked way down here and hiked in. Did you come up Cow Creek Road?"

Nestor nodded and then pointed at the colored marks on the map. "These marks are where you found the bones?"

"I marked, numbered, and recorded the GPS coordinates of everything we've found so far." James pulled his phone out of his pocket. "Do you want to see the pictures?"

"Not yet." Yazzi motioned for him to put the phone away. "But I appreciate your enthusiasm. What's your next move?"

James pointed toward the top of the page. "I figure we should keep following the creek bed north."

"China Dam is only half a mile upstream," Nestor noted. "It's breached, but it's not likely the bodies came past that. They might have been dumped below it."

James studied the map again. "Well, there is another big wash that comes in from the east just before you get up to the dam."

Will stepped forward and injected himself into the conversation. "Are you guys gonna need me for this? I *am* the detective here, remember?"

Nestor didn't look away from the map as he spoke. "If you have something worth saying, say it. Otherwise, let Stray Dog finish."

Encouraged by the deputy's support, James cleared his throat and continued.

"Like I was saying, there's another big wash that comes in from the east—Rich Gulch. It looks like it might flow high enough to carry a body. If we don't find any more signs in the main channel north of it, we should try that direction."

"If you've got four-wheel drive, there's a couple of roads that come in from the east," Will added. "They lead to some old mines in that area. We can get there from Table Mesa Road."

"Might be worth a look," Nestor nodded. "But we're following Stray Dog's plan first. No point in wasting time if we find bones above the gulch."

"We?" Will puffed up as he addressed the deputy. "You're just here to deal with the extra body parts Jimmy and I already found. We've got a fresh homicide to deal with. I'm working for a multi-agency taskforce trying to solve a *new* murder."

"Miller didn't tell you?" Nestor smiled a little bigger this time. "So am I. As long as we're in Yavapai County, you work for me."

Will turned and stomped away half a dozen steps before spinning around and planting his hands on hips. "We're on the same team? *Why*? What the hell do a bunch of old bones have to do with *this* case?"

"Maybe nothing, maybe everything." Nestor's straight-faced expression returned. "That's what we're here to find out. I'm going back to my truck to gear up. Put out that fire and meet me in the creek bed."

James removed some of the stones from one side of the ring and kicked dirt over the remaining coals to smother them, then stirred in some water to finish the job. Will stowed the last of his gear and shouldered his pack. As James reached for his, Will stopped him.

"I've got it." He grunted as he lifted the heavy bundle.

James reached out and tried to take it away. "You don't have to carry my gear."

"A bet's a bet," he said jerking it back. "When I give my word I stick to it."

James put one hand on his brother's shoulder and the other on the pack. "I know, but I don't feel right making you carry everything. I know I just got lucky. I did the research and wrote about how to do it, but I never actually tried it until yesterday."

"Lucky or not, you did it." Will released his grip on the pack. "You certainly impressed that Navajo cop."

"Yeah, right." James slipped his pack on and secured it. "If he's so impressed, why does he keep calling me a stray dog?"

"Coming from him, I'd guess it's a term of affection." Will grinned. "At least he didn't call *you* pigheaded."

Chapter 9

By the time Will and James made their way back to the wash, Deputy Yazzi was already waiting. Nestor pointed at James and then motioned up the channel. "You have the map. Lead the way."

Will stood his ground. "Shouldn't we spread out? We'll find more that way."

"We're heading straight for Stray Dog's wash." Nestor didn't even look back as he started walking. "I called for a CSI team. The evidence technicians will deal with this area when they get here."

Will mumbled something under his breath and fell in behind Nestor. James led them up the creek bed, pointing out any bones he saw along the way. The trio picked their way around boulders and brush, working up the narrowing ravine until they reached the spot they were aiming for.

"This is it." James pointed to a tributary that emptied into the creek from the east. "According to the map, this is Rich Gulch. It's the biggest wash that comes in below China Dam."

Will motioned to the north. "I guess I'll start looking up here toward the dam. You guys can take the gulch."

"No need." Nestor pointed up the side channel. "Your body came down this way."

"And just how do you know that?" Will countered. "Are you psychic, or did your spirit guide tell you?"

Nestor took a few steps into the mouth of the wash. He pulled out his phone and snapped a picture before reaching down to free an object wedged between a couple of rocks. Turning around, he dumped the sand out of a black Nike running shoe, inspected the interior, and then held it up.

"Look familiar?" The deputy waved it in the air before tossing it to Will. "Black Nike, size ten."

"Right shoe." Will looked it over and tossed it back. "Probably his. Dino still had the left one on when we found him."

Nestor put the shoe in an evidence bag and sealed it up. "You're on the right trail, Stray Dog. Lead on, and keep your eyes open."

"Just a minute," Will held up a hand. "We're the trained investigators here. Jimmy's just a civilian. Now that we have the area narrowed down, don't you think one of us should go first?"

"He got you this far. Why do you want to change now?" Nestor asked in his usual monotone. "Would you take off your boots halfway through a thorn patch?"

"Point taken." Will turned to his brother. "You heard the man, Jimmy. Get your boots moving, but be careful. If you screw up any evidence, it's *my* head that's on the chopping block. I'm the one that brought you out here in the first place."

James started making his way up the gulch with Nestor and Will close on his heels. He carefully scanned from side to side as he inched forward, determined not to miss a single clue. No more than thirty yards in, his diligence paid off.

"Up here!" James pointed to a pile of debris a few feet in front of him. "It's a spine, and it still has some ribs connected."

Will leaned in for a closer look. "It's human. I guess this means the other bodies came from this direction, too."

Nestor nodded. "Looks that way."

James tapped his brother on the shoulder. "Um . . .Will?"

"Yeah?"

"Look up there." He pointed to a rusted piece of steel sticking out of the wall of the gulch. "Is that what I think it is?"

"Holy shit Jimmy, I think you just hit the bull's-eye!" Will scrambled forward, followed closely by Nestor. "Yazzi, you got another one of those evidence bags?"

Nestor turned his back toward James. "Lower right pocket. Marker's in there, too."

James retrieved a bag and the marker from Nestor's pack and handed it to him. Deputy Yazzi held the bag open as Will freed a scrap of red cloth from the piece of metal and dropped it in.

"That's his shirt, right?" James was visibly excited. "The color is right and look at the pattern . . . it matches the part he still had on!"

Will tried to calm James as Nestor sealed the bag and labeled it. "Bring it down a notch, Jimmy. We still haven't found where he started his trip."

"But we're getting close," Nestor added pointing out several more objects littering the gully. "More bones and debris. Things are not as spread out. That means we're getting closer to the source."

"Distribution Pattern Analysis," James observed.

Will looked confused. "What the hell are you talking about?"

James held his hands up in a V shape. "It's a typical wedge pattern."

"Exactly." Nestor managed a tiny smile again. "The farther you get from the source, the wider the data points are distributed, the closer you get to the source . . ."

James finished the sentence. "The more concentrated the distribution of points."

"Same principle as blood spatter," Will pointed out. "You could have just said that in the first place."

"He did." Nestor chuckled for the first time. "Maybe you should use smaller words next time, Stray Dog."

Will scowled. "When are you gonna stop taking shots at me?"

"When you stop handing me ammunition." Nestor smiled big enough to show some teeth this time.

"Yeah? Well, load up on this!" Will took a few more steps up the gulch. "Look at the trash mixed in with the bones and rocks." He pointed at a pile of rusted cans, nails and scraps of wood. "And most of the rocks around here have sharp edges . . . not rounded off like you'd expect to see in a creek bed."

"You're right." James picked up a couple of the larger ones and inspected them closer. "These look like they have tool marks."

"Like they came out of a tailings pile, right?" Will turned to Nestor. "I'm betting these bodies were washed out of an old mineshaft."

Nestor nodded his head. "You'd be making a good bet this time."

"If this is somebody's dumping ground, you can also bet they didn't hike in here to do the dumping." Will peered up at the steep walls of the gulch. "Jimmy, get your map out. I want to see how close any vehicle access gets to this place, and there's no way in hell I'm getting a GPS signal down here."

James retrieved the map and looked it over. "It looks like there are a few primitive roads into the area from the east and one from the west. It crosses Humbug Creek north of the dam."

"I think that one was washed out last time Donny and I brought the Jeep up here." Will turned to Nestor.

"Odds are one of those roads leads to an old mine around here."

"There are hundreds of mines in these mountains," Nestor replied. "Every road leads to at least one. We just have to figure out which one is ours."

"I have an idea." James pointed to the map again.

"Go ahead," Will sighed. "Much as I hate to admit it, your track record is looking pretty good right now."

"Well, we know we're getting close, so we should concentrate our efforts in this area." James drew a circle on the map with a pencil.

"Ok," Will replied. "That still leaves a lot of ground to cover."

"I don't think he's done yet." Nestor gave James a wink. "Keep going, Stray Dog."

"If you look at the topography, anything south of this wash would drain downhill and into the next one. That eliminates any of the roads down here." He used the pencil to shade out the lower area of the circle. "If you look at the map, there are only three roads into the search area."

"We can eliminate this one." Will pointed to one of the remaining tracks. "It runs on the east side of the next ridge, so anything on that road would drain into the Agua Fria River."

James shaded out the area east of the ridge. "That leaves one road coming in from the east and the one from the west you said was washed out."

Nestor looked over James' shoulder. "Mind if I take a peek?"

James handed the map over and watched intently as the deputy studied it.

"The east road crosses this wash about three-quarters of a mile up ahead." Nestor handed the map back. "I say we keep moving that way and look for a wash-out on the north side of the gulch. If we don't find one before we hit the road, we double back on top and look for signs up there."

Will nodded. "Sounds like a plan to me."

Nestor looked at James. "What do you think, Stray Dog?"

"Um . . . yeah," James agreed as he stashed the map back in his pocket. "That makes sense. What do you want to do if we find more . . . um . . . parts along the way?"

"Just make a mental note and let them be." Nestor pointed to the north bank of the wash. "What we want is going to be up there."

"But if you *stop* seeing stuff, say something," Will interjected. "It means we've probably gone too far."

Nestor nodded in agreement. The three men started picking their way up the gulch again with Deputy Yazzi leading the march this time. His pace was slow but steady. His eyes never stopped moving. As he worked his way forward, he scanned the gully in front of him top to bottom, and side to side. After a quarter of a mile, he held up his hand and came to a stop.

"No more debris up ahead, but look at this," Nestor pointed to a runoff channel in the left bank of the wash. "Looks like the last of it came from up here."

Will scrambled up the steep wall to a ledge and surveyed the area above. He looked back over his shoulder and gave a thumbs-up.

"Bingo! I see a washed out tailings pile and a hole straight back into the side of the mountain."

Nestor and James worked their way out of the wash as Will approached the old mine to get a better look. A large heap of rocks and debris partially blocked the shaft. One side of the mound was washed away, leaving a trench leading straight down to the gulch. The floor of the horizontal excavation was littered with rusty metal objects, decomposing cloth, and more bones.

"We found our dumping ground." Nestor peered into the opening. "Look at the water line on the walls. The rains must have filled it up until the tailings pile blocking the entrance couldn't hold it anymore and washed out."

"That would've cleaned this place out like flushing a toilet." Will looked back down toward the gulch. "It would have sent our buddy and his companions right down the hill and into the wash."

James studied the surrounding topography. "There would have been enough runoff from around here to have both Rich Gulch and Humbug Creek running high. They could have easily carried a body all the way to the lake."

"Especially a bloated one," Will added. "That sucker would have floated like a cork."

Nestor nodded, still stone-faced. "So the next question is how did the bodies get up here?"

"Well, nobody carried them up that hill on their backs," Will surmised. "And the water that filled the shaft didn't run uphill either."

"Maybe there's another entrance." James fished out his maps again. "Some of the deeper mines would have to have an airshaft coming down from the top. Maybe one of the roads runs above this."

"It'd be easier to dump a body from above," Nestor replied. "Easy for water to run in too."

James showed Nestor the map again. "It looks like one of the roads that comes in from Table Mesa goes right over the top of us."

"And I have a pretty good idea whose dump we found." Will directed Nestor's attention to a rock over the entrance to the shaft. "That mark look familiar to you?"

Nestor and James both looked at the black handprint on the rock face. Nestor nodded. "I've seen this before . . . not good."

"Is that the mark of the Black Legion?" James looked surprised. "I read about them when I was studying the Lost Dutchman Mine, but that's supposed to be in the Superstition Mountains."

"Look a little closer, Jimmy." Will pointed to a green band around the thumb of the print. "The Black Legion is an Apache legend. This is the sign of the Green Legion and they're no legend. They're *very* real!"

Nestor frowned. "And very dangerous."

Chapter 10

"He did what?" Missy released James from her rib-crushing hug and stepped back. "He made you start a fire with *sticks*?"

"He didn't *make* me do it." James smiled as he removed his hat and ran his fingers through his matted hair. "Will bet me I *couldn't* do it. I actually kind of surprised myself when I saw the flame."

Missy grinned. "I'll bet that really pissed him off."

"Yeah, he didn't talk to me the rest of the night. I offered to make dinner for him, but he just ignored me and ate some nasty military rations."

"That sounds like the Will we know and love," Missy said shaking her head. "So overall, how was your first outdoor experience?"

"Camping out was great, better than I imagined when I was writing articles about it." James unbuttoned his shirt and reached down to loosen the laces of his boots. "Watching the sunrise this morning was amazing, but I *really* missed being able to take a shower."

"Go ahead." Missy gave him a quick kiss on the cheek and headed for the kitchen. "I'll make dinner while you get cleaned up. You can tell me all about your big adventure when you smell a little better."

James made his way down the hall to the master bedroom and paused as his hand gripped the doorknob. Almost a full year had elapsed since his mother passed, but he had only recently moved his things from the smaller room across the hall. Missy helped him take down the aging floral wallpaper and apply a fresh coat of paint, but to James it was still his mother's room. He took a deep breath and turned the knob.

As the door swung open, a smile came across his face. A fresh change of clothes sat neatly stacked in a pyramid on the bed. At the bottom was a faded pair of jeans, followed by a perfectly folded grey T-shirt. Clean underwear and a pair of white crew socks completed the structure. His black leather belt lay coiled beside the stack and a pair of black running shoes sat on the floor.

Wow! You've really got that girl trained. Josh sounded surprised as he echoed in James' head. *Are you sure this is the same woman that leaves the bathroom looking like a hurricane just came through?*

"I think it's nice. It says she cares about me."

It tells me she doesn't want you coming out of here wearing a pair of khakis and a button-down shirt. She wants you looking more like Josh and less like James.

"I just spent two days hiking around in the hills and sweating. If she wanted me to be more like you, she would've told me to skip the shower."

That hurts, Jimmy. That really hurts.

James made his way to the bathroom and turned the water on in the shower. He stripped off his clothes and dropped them in the hamper before stepping in and pulling the curtain. Standing motionless under the stream with his eyes closed, he let the warm water cascade over his head and body.

"God, I missed this," he sighed. "I don't know how people existed before indoor plumbing."

After spending more time than usual in the shower, James dressed and made his way back to the dining room. Missy already had the table set and a bottle of wine open. As he sat down, she emerged from the kitchen carrying two large bowls.

"I hope you're good with a chef salad." She placed the bowls on the table and stood behind him, rubbing his shoulders. "After running around in the desert for a couple days I figured you wouldn't want anything hot."

"Good call." James picked up the open bottle and inspected the label. "So, what kind of wine pairs with a salad?"

"It's a Spanish Tempranillo." She sat down as James filled their glasses. "I have to admit I cheated. I looked it up in one of your articles. You said it's supposed to hold up well to the dressing and meat in this kind of salad."

James smiled. "That's not cheating. It's basically the same thing I did. I didn't actually try the wines when I wrote it. I did the research and came to that conclusion based on other people's experience."

"Well, let's see if you were right. Here's to an evening of *real-world* research." Missy raised her glass and took a sip. "So, did you guys find what you were looking for out there?"

"Oh yeah," James replied, "and a whole lot more."

"More? What do you mean?"

"I mean more bodies." James poked at his dinner, pushing it around the bowl without taking a bite. "Actually, it was more body *parts* . . . no whole bodies."

"*Parts?*" Missy put her fork down. "You found *pieces* of bodies?"

"It was mostly skeletal remains, but some still had muscle and tendons attached." James put his fork down as well. "I just ruined your appetite, didn't I."

"Pretty much." Missy stood up, grabbed the wine bottle in one hand, and her glass in the other. She downed the contents of the glass in two large swallows. "Let's move this party to the living room."

James picked up his glass and followed her to the couch. "Sorry I messed up your dinner."

"It's my fault. I asked the question."

James shook his head, "No, it's my fault. I could've told you about something else and saved the gory details for later."

"Well, that door's open now," she said filling her glass again and setting the bottle on the coffee table. "Might as well walk through it. Just how many bodies did you guys find?"

James shrugged his shoulders. "We're not sure yet. The evidence technicians from Yavapai County are still up there. If I had to guess, I'd say at least seven or eight."

"*Seven or eight?*" Missy's eyes bulged as her eyebrows shot up. "How does somebody kill that many people and get away with it?"

"I don't know." James shook his head and took a drink. "Based on the varying degrees of decomposition, we're guessing some of them were killed at different times. They were dumped in an old mineshaft."

Missy shuddered. "That's creepy. I actually threatened to dump Will's body down a mineshaft when he got you arrested."

James smiled. "If you ever do, make sure you find one that won't flood and wash his body down into the lake."

"If I ever kill him, *you're* helping me hide the body." She laid her head on his shoulder and snuggled in close. "I'm just glad you made it home safe. I was worried about you and Will being out there alone. Those mountains are scary enough without body parts lying all over the place."

"We were only alone yesterday." James put his arm around her. "Deputy Yazzi came out this morning. He's from Yavapai County, and part of the same taskforce Will's working with."

"I'll bet he loved that," Missy replied. "Will's not a fan of small town cops."

"Yeah, they had kind of a rough start. He called Will pigheaded."

Missy giggled. "I like him already! How did you get along with him?"

"He's a little hard to read, but I think he likes me." James smiled. "He even gave me a nickname."

"Really?" She sat up and faced James. "Let's hear it."

"He called me Stray Dog . . . you know, because of how I became a part of the Dugan family."

Missy's smile faded. "That sounds more like an insult than a nickname."

"No," James reassured her. "He likes stray dogs. He also treated me with more respect than Will *ever* has. He asked for my opinion on things and then he actually listened."

"He asked for your help? Does he know you're not a cop?"

"He knew as soon as he looked at me, but he didn't seem to have a problem with it. He even gave me his card and said to contact him directly if I think of anything else that might help."

"Did that piss Will off? He's probably been taking credit for your ideas. Who actually found the mine?"

"It was a team effort. Will contributed, too. He's the one that found the handprint."

"The killer left a handprint?" Missy looked confused. "Wouldn't that have been washed away when the mine flooded?"

"It wasn't that kind of a print," James answered. "It was some kind of a sign over the entrance to the shaft—a black handprint with a green band on the thumb."

"What?" Missy jumped up like she had just been poked with a cattle prod. "Are you sure?"

"Yeah, I saw it too." He took Missy's hand and pulled her back down to the couch. "Are you ok? You look like you're about to pass out. Have you seen that sign before?"

"It's the mark of the Green Legion." Her voice was shaking. "I grew up in the Bradshaw Mountains, Jimmy. You don't want to mess with those guys. Promise me you won't go back up there!"

"You know about the Green Legion?" James put his glass down. "Do you know who they are?"

Missy nodded, "I know a couple of them."

"You have names? We need to call Will." James reached for his phone.

"NO!" Missy grabbed the phone from his hand.

James looked puzzled. "Why not? If you have names it might help the investigation."

"I can't, okay?"

"But . . ."

"Drop it, Jimmy!"

James took her hands and pulled her closer again. "You know I can't drop it, so you might as well tell me. Why won't you help? Is it because you don't want to help Will? We can call Deputy Yazzi instead. You can give him the names."

Missy sighed. "I can't, Jimmy. I just can't."

"Why?"

Missy wrapped her arms around her boyfriend and laid her head on his chest. A tear rolled down her cheek as she spoke softly.

"Because I can't rat on family."

Chapter 11

Will Dugan walked through the door of the second floor squad room at the precinct building in downtown Phoenix. He had a tattered messenger bag slung over one shoulder, and a white bag clutched in his hand. The detective made his way across the room and down one of the rows of low walled cubicles. Stopping in front of a cluttered desk, he dropped his messenger bag next to the chair before plopping down in it with a sigh.

Carl Stiverson turned to face his partner. The portly black detective grinned as he leaned forward and reached for the bag.

"Is that what I think it is, Doogie?"

"Breakfast burrito. Potato, egg and chorizo." Will handed it over.

"From Carolina's?"

"That was the bet."

"Ha!" Carl leaned back and opened the bag. "I *told* you the boy could do it! Hell, *I* could probably do it now. You need to stop making fun of that book and read the damn thing."

"Give it a rest, Carl." Will hit the power button on his computer. "I'm not in the mood. I just spent two days listening to Jimmy drone on about his theories and everything else under the sun."

"The kid's smart. I'll put my money on him every time." Carl unwrapped his prize and took a huge bite.

"Apparently, you're not the only one." Will logged on to his computer and started pulling papers out of his satchel. "He impressed that damn Yavapai cop I got saddled with up there."

"They send you some local redneck?" Carl asked between bites.

"Worse." Will put the paperwork down and turned toward his partner. "They sent me some Navajo cop with an attitude . . . Deputy Yazzi. The guy's a pain in the ass."

"Yazzi?" Carl set the burrito down. "His first name doesn't happen to be Nestor, does it?"

"Yeah, Nestor Yazzi." Will looked surprised. "How'd you know that?"

"Well, there ain't that many Navajo cops in Yavapai County, so the odds were pretty heavy in my favor." A big toothy grin lit up on Carl's face. "You're gonna *love* working with that guy!"

"You've worked with him before?"

"Oh yeah. It's been about five years, but you don't forget a guy like that."

Will perked up. "Sounds like you might have the dirt on this guy. Spill it!"

"No dirt, but he's got a hell of a story." Carl leaned back in his chair before continuing. "He might act like he's fresh off the rez, but don't let him fool you . . . that river runs deep."

"How deep?"

Carl raised one eyebrow. "Marine Corp deep."

"A lot of Navajos are Jarheads," Will pointed out. "I had to deal with a bunch of those guys when I was an MP."

Carl's expression grew serious. "How many of those Jarheads spent twelve years in Force Recon?"

"Force Recon?" Will seemed confused. "Are you sure we're talking about the same Yazzi? This guy doesn't fit the mold. He's kinda flat. You know . . . dry."

Carl nodded. "It's the same guy. There's only one Nestor Yazzi, and he's got a hell of a poker face. You ain't gonna get anywhere trying to read that guy, Doogie."

"So, how did you get stuck with him?"

"Like I said, it was about five years ago. He was tracking a couple small time dealers outta Prescott, working up the supply chain. When it led him into town, he landed on my doorstep. I only spent three days with the man, but he left a pretty big impression."

"I was with him for less than a day and I wanted to leave a big impression in his skull," Will said, shaking his head.

"Don't even try." Carl went back to his burrito. "That man could take you down fifty different ways without even thinking about it."

"Alright, so what's the best way to deal with him?"

"You're not gonna like it." Carl's smile grew again. "It's something you ain't good at."

Will leaned back. "Try me."

"Best way to deal with Yazzi is just shut up and listen. You speak up when you got something to contribute, and then you shut up and listen. You'll learn volumes from that man if you give 'im a chance."

"Yeah, I already got the 'shut up if you don't have anything worth saying' lecture." Will slumped down in his chair. "What really twists my shorts is he made some snap judgments about me as soon as he walked into camp. I was fighting against that the rest of the day."

"He's pretty good at sizing people up. What'd he say?"

"He said I was pigheaded and I suck at making bets."

"Give the man a gold star!" Carl held up what was left of his burrito in a mock salute. "He wasn't wrong."

"I'm not pigheaded. I'm *determined*."

"No, you're pigheaded," Carl replied. "It's one of the things that makes you a good cop. Once you get your teeth into something, you don't like to let go . . . even when you're wrong. From what I've seen, you get that from your mama."

"Well, I'm keeping my teeth in this case." Will turned back to his desk. "I still can't believe what we found up there yesterday."

"Freaked me out a little too when I got your message." Carl shuddered. "I've heard some stories about those mountains, but damn . . ."

"Did you dig anything up on Romero's old partner while I was gone?"

Carl pulled a file out of his drawer and handed it across the aisle. "Bernard Bennett, AKA Bam-Bam. Don't bother looking for him at the last known address. I swung by there yesterday. It's a burned-out crack house. According to the neighbors, the place has been abandoned since a fire went through it six months ago."

"Six months . . . that's right after we busted his boss." Will opened the file and studied a few pages. "The timing's a little convenient."

Carl nodded. "I thought the same thing. You figure he torched the place to get rid of anything connecting him to Albert Bernstein?"

"Maybe, but check this out." Will grabbed a piece of paper off the pile on his desk and held it up. "Dino gave the same address last time he was busted, but it doesn't match his driver's license. I don't think either one of them were living there."

Carl swallowed the last bite of his breakfast before replying. "Must be some reason they both gave that address."

"That's what I'm thinking." Will rubbed at the stubble on his chin. "They both worked for Bernstein, maybe it was one of his drop houses. Dino and Bam-

Bam could have set the fire to destroy evidence. It might be worth a trip back out there."

"I poked through it yesterday. There's nothing left in there but trash and old needles."

Will handed the file back to Carl. "Then I'll head over to the address on Dino's license and work from there."

"I'll see if I can chase down Bennett." Carl opened the folder and looked it over again. "He's got a sister in the area. I'll look her up. If we get lucky, maybe we can locate Bam-Bam and get a lead . . . if he's still alive."

Will turned his chair to face Carl. "I hadn't thought of that. He could be one of the other bodies we found."

"They could've been working together again. Maybe ended up in the same hole, too."

"No, Dino was the only fresh body we found. If Bennett was there too, he had to be killed earlier . . . much earlier based on the condition of the other remains. All we can do is look for him and hope he's still breathing. He's our best lead right now."

"Maybe, but I've been thinking about another angle too."

Will's eyes lit up as he leaned forward. "Did you find something else?"

"No, but I see a few things starting to line up in one general direction."

"What direction is that?"

"Think about it." Carl drummed his fingers on the Bennett file lying on his desk. "These two worked for Bernstein when we busted him. Right after the sting, a house they're both tied to—maybe tied to Bernstein too—gets torched."

"Right." Will settled back into his chair. "What's your point?"

"Who did these guys blame for their boss getting caught?"

Will threw up his hands and spun back toward his desk. "You're not going there again, are you?"

"The hell I'm not!" Carl pointed at a composite drawing taped to the front of his file cabinet. "Somebody had to come in and fill the gap when we took Al off the street."

"It's not him, Carl. Nobody's seen the guy since then."

"Maybe he hasn't been seen, but his name comes up a lot."

"Yeah, because of those two idiots!" Will pointed at the file under Carl's fist. "They turned him into an urban legend. He was just a drug mule. Let it go."

"A mule doesn't disappear from custody in the middle of the night, especially when he wasn't caught holding," Carl pointed out. "He'd just ask for a lawyer and keep his mouth shut. He had to know he'd be back on the street in no time."

"Maybe he had priors or an outstanding warrant. He got outta here before you had a chance to process him."

"I thought about that," Carl replied. "That's why I dusted the table in the interview room after he scooted."

Will felt a knot form in his stomach. "Did you get any clean prints?"

"Yeah." Carl smirked. "Over forty different ones. Somebody needs to wipe those tables down a little more often. They're almost as nasty as your desk."

Will breathed an internal sigh of relief. "So, nothing useable?"

"Almost every one of them came back to known suspects."

"Almost?" Will tightened up again.

"Yeah, the rest were all cops."

Will finally relaxed. "So, what you're saying is you're no closer to this clown than you were six months ago. Give it up Carl, he's not our guy."

"My gut says he is. I've been waiting all year for this man to poke his head up and I think he just did." Carl closed one eye, extended his thumb and aimed his index finger at the face in the sketch.

"I've got you in my sights, *Jimmy Ray!*"

Chapter 12

Will stood on the front stoop of the pale-yellow house in the Willo Historic District of downtown Phoenix. He pounded on the big wooden door and rang the bell several times before finally giving up. He pulled out his cell phone and dialed his brother's number.

"Jimmy, where the hell are you?"

"I'm at home," the voice on the other end of the line answered. "Where are you?"

"I'm on your front porch. I've been beating on the door for the last ten minutes. Didn't you hear me?"

"No, if I heard you I would have let you in. I'm out in the garage."

Will shoved the phone back in his pocket and walked around the side of the house. The detached garage sat about twenty feet behind the main structure. A roll-up door opened to the alley running behind the row of restored and renovated homes. A sandstone path made its way across the yard, terminating at the side entry to the garage. Will twisted the knob and pushed the door. He stood in the opening for a moment, looking around.

"Shut the door, please." James pointed at a thermostat over the workbench. "You're running up the air conditioning bill."

"You have AC in your garage?" Will stepped in and kicked the door shut behind him. "Talk about spoiled."

"How else am I supposed to work out here in the summer?" James sat on a stool flipping through the pages of an auto repair manual. "My father installed an evaporative cooler when he built this place but it doesn't really do the job when the humidity gets high, so I upgraded."

"A little sweat never hurt anybody." Will stepped toward the faded blue vehicle backed into the garage. "What the hell is this?"

"It's a Land Rover."

"I can see it's a Land Rover."

James shrugged. "Okay, it's a right-hand drive, 1974 Series III Land Rover."

"What I meant was what the hell are *you* doing with it?"

"I can't keep borrowing your Jeep every time I have to make a dramatic entrance as Josh, so I'm fixing this up."

"*You're* fixing this pile of junk?" Will snickered. "All by yourself?"

"He's got help." Missy's head poked out from under the hood of the car.

"What are you, chief parts washer?" Will snickered. "What do you know about cars?"

"More than you do." Missy walked up to Will, wiping her hands on a rag. "I couldn't afford to take my car to a mechanic, so I had to work on it myself."

"I guess that explains why you don't have a car anymore."

"You think you could have fixed it, smart guy?" She reached up and stuffed the greasy rag in his shirt pocket.

Will pulled the rag out and tossed it on the bench next to James. "I can fix damn near anything."

"Oh, really?" Missy planted her hands on her hips. "My old Chevy threw a connecting rod out the side of the engine block. Think you could have fixed that?"

"Sure," Will replied. "It would have taken me half a day to pull the old engine out and stuff in a new one."

"I could've done that too if I had the money, but it would have cost me $1200 for a new short-block."

"I would've hit the junkyard."

"The junkyard wanted $800 for a used engine—I only had $200. I got a $500 tax write-off when I donated the rust-bucket, so I figure I came out ahead."

Will put his hand out and leaned on the Rover. "So, you think wrenching on that old Chevy qualifies you to work on British cars? These things are pretty temperamental."

"Well, it wouldn't start when we rolled it in here yesterday." Missy ducked under Will's arm and walked around to the right side of the vehicle. "Let's see what happens now."

She slid into the driver's seat, pumped the accelerator a couple of times, and turned the key. The starter clunked and let out a grinding noise that built into a whine as it picked up speed. The engine coughed, sputtered, and backfired a few times before finally catching. Missy throttled it up for a few seconds before allowing the engine to settle down to a rough idle.

James jumped to his feet. "You got it running!"

Will opened the door and fanned the thick exhaust smoke with his hand. "Yeah, running like crap."

"I'm not done yet." Missy shut the engine off and walked back around the rear of the car. "I still have to set the timing and adjust the carburetor. When I'm done, Nigel's gonna be purring like a kitten."

"*Nigel?*" Will laughed as he looked at James. "You named your car *Nigel*?"

"Missy named it. I wanted to call it Bruce, but she didn't think that sounded British enough."

Will rubbed his forehead. "You're both crazy, but I didn't come over here to meet Nigel . . . or Bruce—whatever you call that thing. I need to talk to you about the Romero case."

James shut the door before dropping back onto his stool. He closed the manual on the counter and looked at Will. "Did you figure out who killed him?"

"I'd say the Green Legion is still a pretty good bet." Will pulled up another stool and sat down. "But we haven't identified anybody specific yet."

"What is the Green Legion?" James asked. "I couldn't find any information about them online."

"They're a group of marijuana growers. They have fields hidden all over the Bradshaws."

James glanced in Missy's direction. "So, you don't know who any of the members are?"

Missy remained silent.

"No," Will said, shaking his head. "They're up in Yazzi's territory, so he's running down that angle. I'm more interested in what our buddy Dino was doing up there in the first place."

James fidgeted on his stool. "Why do need you to talk to me about it?"

"Because you're a suspect."

Missy and James both reacted in unison. "*WHAT?*"

Will let out a huge laugh as he doubled over and slapped his leg. "Just kidding! Carl's looking at *Jimmy Ray* as a suspect, but we both know he's not getting anywhere heading down that trail."

Missy balled her hand into a tight fist and cocked her arm back. Putting all of her weight behind the punch, she connected with the surprised detective's shoulder, sending him spinning off his stool. Will hit the concrete floor with a thud.

"You nearly gave both of us a heart attack, you *dumbass*!" She hauled back and kicked him in the thigh before turning to James. "Sorry, I know I promised I'd stop calling him that."

"I think we can make an exception this time." James smiled and reached down to offer his brother a hand—Will swatted it away.

"I can get myself up. Just call off your guard dog."

"She's not my guard dog, and you know you deserved that."

"Okay, maybe I did." Will dusted himself off and remounted his stool. "Let's get back on topic."

"So, why do you need to talk to me about this?" James asked again.

"We'll get to that in a minute." Will rubbed his shoulder as he spoke. "Let me catch you up on where we stand first."

James nodded, but didn't say a word. Missy glared in silence at Will as she stood next to her boyfriend with her arm around him.

"I've been trying to figure out the last time anyone saw Dino, and who he was working for when he disappeared. I'm not having a whole lot of luck."

"Have you tried to find the other guy that was with him at the coffee shop?" James asked. "Maybe he knows."

"Bam-Bam? Yeah, we chased down that lead. At first, we thought he might have been one of the other bodies from the mine, but Carl found him hiding out at his sister's place down by South Mountain."

"Did he tell you anything?"

Will shook his head. "Carl couldn't get a damn thing out of him. I'm sure he's got information, but he's not about to spill it to a cop. We don't have anything on him to use for leverage and he knows it."

James looked puzzled. "I still don't know why you're telling me all of this."

"Just hold on," Will replied. "I'm getting there."

"Get there faster," Missy interjected with a scowl.

"Like I said," Will continued, "we don't have any leverage on Bennett."

"Who's Bennett?" James asked.

"Bam-Bam is Bernard Bennett—that's his real name. Anyway, he's not afraid of the cops, so we need to find something he *is* afraid of to get him to talk. That's where you come in."

James still looked confused. "How am I supposed to help with that? I don't know what he's afraid of."

"Well, I know one thing Bam-Bam is *definitely* afraid of." Will reached out and poked James in the chest. "*You!*"

"Me?" James looked surprised. "Why would he be afraid of me? I don't even know the guy!"

"But he knows you. Or more precisely, he knows Jimmy Ray."

"Oh, no!" Missy's face turned red as she clenched her fist and stepped toward Will. "You're not putting him in the middle of *that* shit again!"

"Hold on, Missy." James caught her around the waist and held her back. "Let me get this straight, you want me to play Jimmy Ray again?"

"Yup."

"And intimidate information out of a professional bodyguard who outweighs me by at least fifty pounds?"

"You got it."

"Just how do you propose I do that?"

"You're Jimmy Ray—he's already afraid of you. Besides, you'll have backup muscle of your own."

Missy slipped out of James' grip. "Who's going to back him up? Every cop in town is on the lookout for Jimmy Ray, so you can't use undercover officers."

"I'll back him up. My Willy-D cover is still intact."

"I thought your cover was a drug dealer, not hired muscle." James responded.

"Good cover is deeper than that, Jimmy. I set Willy-D up as a former Army Ranger, kicked out for drug smuggling. I can play him as a dealer or an enforcer."

"What about your partner?" Missy interjected. "If there's another Jimmy Ray sighting, he's going to be all over it."

"I can handle Carl." Will addressed James again. "So, what do you say? You up for it?"

James looked at Missy and then leaned in close to Will. "Have you been getting into Mom's private stock again?"

Chapter 13

James paced back and forth in the dark alley next to the seedy South Phoenix bar while Will kept watch. The unshaven detective was dressed in faded jeans, a sleeveless T-shirt, and black military boots. He peeked around the corner of the building every few seconds, and then quickly retracted his head before he could be seen.

"I can't believe I'm doing this." James chewed on his nails as he walked. "I'm worried about playing Jimmy Ray again. What if I mess up? Are you sure there's no other way?"

"Relax, you can handle this." Will leaned up against the graffiti covered wall and crossed his arms. "Just do whatever you need to do to get into character . . . you know, like when you have to play Josh."

"I *drink* when I have to play Josh!"

"Yeah, that's probably not a good idea tonight. You need to be one hundred percent on your game." Will stepped forward and put his hands-on James' shoulders, stopping him mid-stride. "Listen, I wouldn't ask you to do this if I didn't think you had it in you. You did fine the last time. I know you can do it again."

"I barely said anything last time. I just looked at the guy and nodded a lot." James brushed Will's hands off and resumed his nervous march.

"I'm afraid that's not gonna work in this situation. If we're gonna get this guy to talk, you have to intimidate him. You have to really make him squirm."

James stopped and glared at his brother. "And just how do you propose I do that?"

"Well, the pissed off look on your face right now is a great start. I'd hold on to that."

James pointed at his face with both hands. "This look isn't anger, it's *fear*! What if I can't intimidate him? Worse yet, what if he decides to just go ahead and *shoot* me or something?"

"Relax, Bro, I'll have your back." Will peeked around the corner again. "He should be coming by here any time now. Carl said Bennett hits this bar about the same time every night."

"That's the other thing I don't get. Why are we doing this out here?" James pointed down the alley. "He could just turn and run when he sees us. Wouldn't it be better to corner him inside where he can't get away?"

"Never jump a guy on his home turf, Jimmy," Will replied, still looking around the corner of the building. "If he's a regular in this dive, you can bet some of the *other* regulars are gonna step in if shit gets real."

James shook his head. "This isn't real, it's *surreal*!"

"Well, whatever it is you'd better get your game face on. Here he comes." Will pulled a small revolver from a concealed holster inside his waistband and palmed it. He turned back toward James.

"Pull yourself together and hang back here until I stop him. I'll give you a signal when I want you to come out."

James stepped back into the shadows. "What's the signal?"

"You'll know when you see it," Will replied. "Just pay attention."

A muscular, dark haired man made his way down the empty sidewalk, keeping his head low as he passed under a dim streetlight. When he was close to the alley, Will stepped out and into his path, arms hanging at his sides. The man stopped dead and lifted his head, staring directly into Will's eyes.

"Who the hell are you?" Bennett rested a hand on his bulging pocket.

Will turned his right hand forward, revealing the gun seated firmly in his palm. "No need for that, Bam-Bam."

Bennett moved his hand away from his side. "Okay, so you know my name . . . do I know you?"

"Name's Willy-D."

"Never heard of you."

"I'm pretty sure you've heard of my boss." Will stepped to the side and motioned to his brother.

A rush of adrenaline surged through James' veins. He moved out of the alley, wearing the same blank expression he had the night of the drug sting. Bennett stood silent, studying the young man's face. After a few seconds, his eyes grew wide and he took a step back. James straightened up and stood a little taller, trying as best he could to take advantage of the moment by appearing larger.

"You're Jimmy Ray." Bennett seemed to shrink as the words came out of his mouth. "I remember you from that night . . . in the coffee shop."

"When Marco got arrested," James said firmly.

"Yeah, when Marco went down. You set that up?"

James crossed his arms across his chest. "What do *you* think?"

Bennett looked at the gun in Will's hand, and then back at James. "I think I don't like this situation. Waddaya want from me?"

Josh lit up in James' brain. *Let the sparring begin!*

"Information," James growled.

"What if I don't have the information you're looking for?"

James lowered his chin and raised one eyebrow. "That might be a problem."

Bennett took another step back. Will quickly moved behind him, cutting off his exit.

"Where ya goin', Bam-Bam?" An evil smile grew on Will's face. "Conversation's not over yet."

James took a step forward and stared into Bennett's eyes. "Did you hear about your friend Dino?"

Nice footwork.

"I ain't seen him around lately. Word on the street is he might be . . ." Bennett swallowed hard, ". . . dead."

James held his unflinching stare. "The street is correct."

Yeah! Give him a little jab!

"Did you . . ."

"No," James cut him off. "But I intend to find out who did."

"Why do *you* care who killed Dino?"

"I don't care about Dino." James was really getting into his role. "What I *do* care about is the competition. Who was Dino working for when he disappeared?"

Ah, hit him with a quick combo!

"I . . . I don't know," Bennett stammered.

"I call *bullshit*," Will snarled from behind. "You two were joined at the hip. I'll bet you're working for the same people as Dino."

"Willy-D's right." James took a deep breath, expanding his chest. "You're lying. I don't like it when people lie to me."

Keep the pressure on him, Jimmy.

"I ain't working for *nobody* right now, I swear! After Dino disappeared, I figured I better lay low for a while."

"You're not too bright." James let the corners of his mouth turn up slightly. "Staying with family, and going to the same bar every night—that isn't lying low.

You were *very* easy to find. I heard some cop even found you."

And the kid lands one below the belt!

"How'd you know that?"

"I have my sources."

"That's how you escaped that night ain't it." Bennett rocked nervously. "You got somebody on the inside."

James narrowed his eyes. "*I'm* asking the questions here. Who was Dino working for?"

That's it, keep him in the corner.

Bennett looked around, and then at the ground in front of his feet. "Well I didn't tell that cop nothin', and I got nothin' to say to you either."

James stood silent for a few seconds, analyzing the man in front of him. He had to have a weakness—something that could be exploited. An evil smile crossed James' face as an idea took hold.

"Okay, maybe we should have a talk with your sister instead."

Jeez, Jimmy, now you're scaring me!

Bennett's eyes snapped back up to meet James'. "You leave my sister outta this! She don't know a *damn* thing!"

"She doesn't know what you do for a living?"

"*Hell* no!"

"You've been hiding out at her house." James leaned one shoulder against the weathered brick wall. "I'm sure she's overheard a few conversations."

"No way. I always take my calls outside so she doesn't hear me."

"Oh, I'm sure she's picked up a thing or two." James looked at his brother. "What do you think, Willy-D?"

"I think you might be on to something, Jimmy Ray." Will grabbed the back of Bennett's collar. "How 'bout it, Bam-Bam? Should we go for a little walk? I'd *love* to meet the family."

"All right, dammit!" Bennett held up his hands. "I'm dead if I talk and dead if I don't, but you gotta keep my sister outta this. She's all the family I got."

James straightened up and approached Bennett again. "Your sister's safe . . . as long as you don't lie to me again."

"Ronny Perez," Bennett said staring at the ground. "We were riding shotgun for Ronny Perez when Dino fell off the map."

"You sure about that?" Will still had a firm grip on the man's collar. "I heard Ronny was doing five years in the state pen down in Florence."

"He made parole in three," Bennett replied. "He's working outta Sunnyslope now—body shop off Seventh Avenue."

James smiled and took a step back. "If you're lying, we'll be back."

Will looked at James and winked. "Are we done with our boy here?"

James gave a small nod. "Let him go."
Holy shit, Jimmy! You did it!

As soon as Will released his grip, Bennett bolted for the door of the bar and disappeared inside. The brothers strode back down the musty alley toward an old Ford Crown Victoria. Will holstered his gun, and then playfully punched James in the shoulder.

"Where in the *hell* did all that come from? You've been holdin' out on me, Bro!"

"What do you mean? I just tried to be intimidating like you said."

"Oh come on, you were a stone-cold badass back there." Will poked at him again. "And the sister thing—that was pure genius!"

"I saw a vulnerability, so I figured I should try to exploit it."

"Exploit it?" Will laughed. "Oh yeah, you exploited it all right. The son-of-a-bitch almost *pissed* himself!"

"*I* almost pissed myself!" James slid into the passenger seat and closed the door as Will jumped in the other side and started the car.

"Well, you didn't let it show. You played that guy like a pro, Jimmy. Built him up slow, and then went in for the kill!"

"That wasn't me. It was all fear and adrenaline."

Will grinned as he slipped the car into gear. "Whatever it was, remember how you did it. You're gonna need to tap into that again when we talk to Perez."

"We?" James' eyes almost popped out of his head. "You're making me do this *again*?"

"Like Yazzi said, you got us this far, why change now?"

"*Now* you're listening to Deputy Yazzi?" James sunk back into the seat. "I thought you didn't like him."

"I don't have to like him to respect him. A wise man once told me if you shut up and listen, you might learn something."

"Did your father tell you that?"

"Nope," Will grinned. "My partner, Carl."

"Yeah, that's going to be another problem. What are you going to do about Carl? You know word's going to get around that Jimmy Ray is back. He's going to be all over that."

"You just leave him to me, Jimmy. I got him off your ass before, I can do it again." Will pulled out onto the street and headed north. "Right now, I think I owe you a drink."

James stared out the window. "I think you owe me several."

Chapter 14

Carl Stiverson sat at his desk in the squad room reading through Will's report from his encounter with Bernard Bennett. He set the file down and looked across the aisle at his disheveled partner.

"I couldn't get two words outta that guy. How'd you get him to talk?"

"I didn't." A toothy grin spread across Will's face. "Willy-D did."

"You used your deep cover? That explains the lack of personal hygiene. You know, it wouldn't have killed you to take a shower before you came in this morning." Carl settled back in his chair with a sigh. "I'll bet you went off without backup again, didn't you? I've warned you about that shit, Doogie. You don't go out on the streets like that without letting me know."

Will shook his head. "Sorry, but I couldn't take the chance on this one Carl. You just questioned Bennett a couple days ago. He knows who you are. If he caught sight of you, we would've lost him."

Carl leaned forward and shook his finger in Will's direction. "I could'a sent somebody else out there to back you up. I'm telling you, Doogie, this damn Lone Ranger shit's gonna get you killed one of these days."

"Come on man, you know I can handle myself without a babysitter," Will scoffed. "Besides, I took someone with me to up the intimidation factor a little."

"You recruited some low-level street muscle?"

Will shifted his eyes away from his partner. "Something like that. Anyway, it worked. We got a name out of him."

Carl turned to his computer and banged on a few keys. "What Bennett told you was right, Renaldo Perez got out almost a year ago. According to the parole report, he's not just working at that body shop, he lives there. His uncle owns the place. Ronny's living in a trailer out back. His job is listed as Night Watchman."

"More like night *salesman*," Will quipped. "If Dino *was* killed by a member of the Green Legion, that means Perez is probably running weed out of the shop. If we can find out who he was buying from, that might give us a solid lead."

Carl picked up the file again. "You send this to Miller yet?"

"Yeah, I emailed him a copy this morning," Will replied. "He called just before you got in. He said the forensic team from Yavapai County is still up on the mountain bagging and tagging. So far they've got at least seven distinct bodies and a pretty good pile of extra parts."

"And they're still collecting evidence?" Carl shook his head and handed the file back to Will. "It's gonna take a couple years and a whole lot of DNA testing to sort that mess out. They find any more wallets laying around?"

"No, I think we just got lucky finding Dino's. Apparently, McCarthy hasn't burned through all that good karma he's got banked up." Will rolled his eyes. "Shit just seems to fall right in his lap."

"So I guess that means no IDs on any of the other bodies yet?"

"Nope. Miller's got his team pulling missing persons reports for the last few years to see if they can match something up, but if these guys were in the same business as Dino, I'm betting most of them weren't reported."

"Maybe they'll get a few hits," Carl replied. "The Legion has fields hidden all over those mountains. Some of those bodies could be people who just wandered into the wrong place."

"Yeah, back before I joined the force Donny and I blew a tire on the Jeep up there when we were four-wheeling." Will leaned back in his chair and chuckled. "When we got back into town, I took the tire into the shop. They found a hole in the sidewall and a 7.62-millimeter full metal jacket slug rolling around inside. I figured it was a warning shot, so we never went back up that particular canyon again."

"Good call. Those boys up there don't mess around." Carl leaned back as well and folded his arms across his barrel-chest. "So, what's your next move? You gonna go back up the mountain to look for Legion members?"

"No, that's Yazzi's area. He's sniffing around the Bradshaw communities for leads." Will raised an eyebrow and gave Carl a sideways look. "I'm not heading back into his territory until I absolutely have to."

"Well I'll be damned!" Carl sat up and smiled at Will. "Looks like we finally found someone who intimidates the great Detective William Dugan!"

"He doesn't intimidate me, Carl. I just don't like his attitude."

"That's not an attitude Doogie, that's knowledge and years of experience."

"Whatever it is, I don't feel like dealing with him right now. I have enough on my plate."

"So, that leaves Ronny Perez."

Will nodded. "Yup. I figure I'll stake out the body shop for a couple of days and see what I can dig up there."

"Sounds solid. If you can catch him violating his parole, that should give you enough leverage to pry his mouth open."

"I don't know about that." Will looked pensive as he ran his fingers through his disheveled hair. "Guys like Ronny aren't afraid to do a couple more years when the alternative is turning somebody like a Legion member in. Alive in prison looks a whole lot better than dead at the bottom of a mineshaft."

"You're not thinking Witness Protection are you?" Carl shook his head. "Good luck selling that one to the Marshalls."

"Nah, I'm not even going to try."

Carl frowned. "You're dragging Willy-D out again?"

Will shrugged his shoulders. "It worked on Bam-Bam, didn't it?"

"Bam-Bam is an idiot," Carl replied. "He's just muscle with nothing between the ears. Perez is going be a tougher nut to crack."

Will smiled. "I just have to use the right nutcracker. I don't think intimidation is gonna work, but maybe dangling a carrot in front of him will."

Carl looked confused. "I don't get it. What do you plan on using for a carrot?"

"Here's my idea." Will leaned toward his partner and lowered his voice. "The Legion took out one of his guys, so he might be up for a little payback. Perez may not want to talk to the cops, but that doesn't mean he won't give up a name if somebody else is willing to do the dirty work."

"So you're gonna offer to be his hit-man?" Carl screwed up his face. "I don't like it. Willy-D is supposed to be a small-time dealer, not a killer. Besides, if word got out he hired somebody to take out a Legion member, he'd be just as dead as if he'd pulled the trigger himself."

"I never said I'd get him to *hire* me," Will replied. "I'm going to offer to do it for free."

"For free?" Carl laughed out loud. "What makes you think he's gonna buy a small-time dope dealer offering to do a murder for free?"

"Listen, word's getting around about all the bodies we found in that hole, right?" Will straightened back up and grinned. "All I have to do is convince Perez that I lost a man up there too . . . you know, show him we're on the same side and give him a reason to share information with me."

Carl rubbed the back of his neck and thought for a moment before responding. "And if he doesn't bite?"

"Then we try it your way," Will conceded. "You can still bust him for trafficking and offer him a deal if he rolls on his supplier."

"I thought you said he wouldn't go for that."

"And I don't think he will. That's why my way *has* to work."

Carl nodded. "Fine, but you ain't going in there without proper backup this time."

"We'll talk about it when the time comes." Will spun his chair back around to face his computer. "I've got to stake him out first and confirm what he's dealing. If it is pot, we're probably barking up the right tree."

"Well, you can't do that alone either," Carl said sternly. "I'm riding shotgun."

"I can't have you with me, Carl. You've busted Perez before, he knows you. Hell, you've been taking these guys down for twenty years—*everybody* knows you."

"Okay, then I'll see if I can get Officer Marquez." Carl picked up his phone. "He's been itching to get out of that uniform and do a little undercover work."

"Jesse?" Will grimaced. "Come on man, he's too clean-cut. He'll get spotted right away."

Carl shook his head. "He'll be fine. He's just gotta sit in a damn car and keep you awake."

"I'm not going to be sitting in a car looking like a cop, Carl. I'll stick out like a sore thumb." Will turned back to face his partner. "In that neighborhood, I can play homeless and nobody will look twice at me. There's an alley running behind the shop. Ronny's trailer is right up against the chain-link fence. It's the perfect setup. Just give me a shopping cart and cardboard box, and I'm golden."

"Great." Carl lowered his head and stared at Will from under a raised eyebrow. "But you still ain't doing this alone. I'll tell Jesse to hit Goodwill on his way home and skip the showers after his workout."

Chapter 15

A hot breeze tossed a plastic bag down the dusty alley. It rolled past a shopping cart with several flattened cardboard boxes resting on sticks bridged between its handle and the rusty chain link fence. Two tattered figures settled into their makeshift shelter as the sun dipped low in the August sky.

Officer Jesse Marquez couldn't contain his excitement. "So, what's the plan? This is my first undercover stakeout."

"The plan?" Detective Dugan settled back against the fence. "The plan is to wipe that smile off your face and look like the rest of the bums around here. A happy homeless guy tends to draw unwanted attention. Just relax, and keep your eyes and ears open."

Jesse sat cross-legged facing Will and straightened out his expression. He tried his best to not look too obvious as he scanned the gravel lot on the other side of the fence. Half a dozen cars in various states of repair were lined up on one side of the open garage door on the back of the building. Piles of crushed and twisted metal were strewn around the area as well. A faded aluminum travel trailer sat perpendicular to the fence; its front door was no more that fifteen feet from Will's back.

"It looks like they might be getting ready to close up, Sir." Jesse nonchalantly slid his sleeve up to sneak a look at his watch. "It's almost six o'clock."

"Drop the *sir*, Jesse. We're just two homeless guys settling in for the night, remember? And quit checking your watch, it's kind of a dead giveaway. Perez isn't open for business yet, so we've got some time."

"Sorry . . . Will." The young officer finally relaxed his posture and extended his legs, leaning back against the cart. "Thanks for agreeing to let me do this. I really appreciate the opportunity."

Will shrugged his shoulders. "Carl didn't give me much of a choice. He hates it when I fly solo."

Jesse's eyes widened. "You were planning on going in there to arrest this guy with no backup?"

Will shook his head. "We're not arresting anybody tonight. We're just here to get a line on this guy—see what he's dealing and, if we're lucky, who he's dealing with."

Jesse noticed a thin wire running out from under Will's collar. It was connected to a small bud tucked into the detective's left ear.

"Did you plant a listening device? Are you recording his conversations?"

"Huh?" Will looked confused for a moment before remembering the wire. "Oh, the earpiece. Nah, that's for my phone. Mom has a bad habit of calling at the wrong time and I don't want it ringing out loud."

"Your mom does that too?" Jesse smiled. "Mine calls at least three times every shift just to make sure I'm still alive. If I don't answer right away, she freaks out and calls my sergeant."

"I'll bet she passed out when you told her you're going undercover."

Jesse lowered his head in mock shame. "I didn't tell her."

Will chuckled. "Good plan."

Jesse remained silent, watching over Will's shoulder as a man came around the corner of the building. He pulled the gate to the yard closed and locked it, then stepped inside the garage door and rolled it down. The yard was empty again, leaving the two men free to talk once more.

"So, why aren't we recording this?" Jesse asked. Don't we need it to prove what the suspect is doing?"

"We can't." Will reached into a paper sack sitting on the ground next to him, pulling out a bottle of water and an energy bar. "That's private property. Without a warrant, or the owner's permission, we can't plant a mic or camera on the premises."

"Reasonable expectation of privacy," Jesse sighed. "That could taint the evidence."

Will nodded as he opened the bottle and took a drink. "Exactly, but there's no law that says we can't sit here on public property and watch the world go by. If somebody's voice happens to carry, or we see something illegal through the fence . . ."

"Then we have probable cause for a warrant."

"Right," Will responded. "But that's not the primary goal today. We need to verify what this guy is dealing. If I'm right, his supply chain is going to lead us back up the mountain, and right to whoever killed Romero."

Jesse looked puzzled. "Who's Romero?"

"Carl didn't tell you about Dino?"

"Detective Stiverson told me I was backing you up while you were staking out a dealer. He never said anything about a homicide."

"I can't believe he sent you out here cold." Will shook his head and took a bite of his energy bar. "I'll give you the back-story later. Right now, we need to find out if Perez is dealing weed. If he is, I'm betting he's getting it out of the Bradshaws."

"You think he's dealing with the Green Legion?" Jesse lowered his eyes and crossed himself. "¡Madre de Dio!"

Will laughed at the officer's reaction. "I guess that means you've heard of the Legion."

"I ran into a couple of those guys last year." Jesse's eyes started to light up as he talked. "I stopped a car for running a red light and smelled alcohol on the driver, so I detained him. When he failed the field sobriety test, he was desperate to call someone to come get his car. He got really belligerent about it, so I had the vehicle towed to impound."

"Had something in there he didn't want you to find?"

"Oh, yeah." Jesse smiled and nodded. "One of the canine units happened to be there when the tow truck pulled into the lot. His dog came totally unglued when the car went by. They found over a hundred pounds of marijuana in the trunk, all stamped with a black handprint and a green thumb-band."

Will nodded. "That's the Legion's mark. You don't happen to remember the guy's name, do you?"

"I don't remember the driver's name." Jesse took a deep breath. "But I sure remember the uncle he called to bail him out. He was really pissed off—I mean *scary* mad. I thought the guy was going to explode when I told him we couldn't release the car—threatened everybody in the whole place. He didn't seem to care about his nephew, just the car. He denied it, but he knew exactly what was in the trunk."

"He was more worried about his product than his own family?" Will grinned." Oh yeah, he knew."

"When he saw the kid, he called him every name in the book and a few I've never heard before. The uncle left without even offering to post the guy's bail."

"What was the uncle's name?"

Jesse thought for a moment. "It was Franklin."

Will sat up straight. "Franklin? Are you sure?"

"Yeah, Walter Franklin."

"Do you remember where the kid was from?"

Jesse shook his head. "I don't recall, but I know it took quite a while for his uncle to get here. Once I did some research and learned about the Green Legion, I assumed he came from up in the Bradshaws somewhere. Do you think this guy might be connected to your homicide?"

"I don't know, but that's the first name I've actually heard connected to this group." Will looked down and mumbled to himself. "I also know a Franklin that has family up there."

Jesse gave no indication he heard Will's answer. His focus had shifted to the thin, dark-haired man coming out the back door of the body shop and walking toward the trailer. His dirty coveralls were rolled down from the top with the arms tied around his waist. A dingy white tank top left his heavily tattooed arms exposed, the crude artwork scrawled in prison-green.

Jesse tapped Will's foot to get his attention and gave a slight nod in the man's direction. "This looks like Perez," he whispered.

"It's show time, kid." Will turned his head to the right, positioning his open ear toward the trailer. "Keep your eyes open and your mouth closed."

Ronny Perez made his way across the yard to the trailer, paying no attention to the two men on the other side of the fence. Like the rest of homeless people that made their camps on the canal banks and in the alleys, they might as well have been invisible. As Perez reached the door of the trailer, the phone in his hand began broadcasting a loud mariachi tune.

"What's up?" Perez paused for a moment and leaned against the trailer, pressing the phone to his ear. "Same as last time? Yeah, I can cover that. No, give me twenty minutes to grab a shower and I'll meet you at the gate."

Ronny pocketed the phone and stepped inside the trailer, pulling the door closed behind him. The corners of the detective's mouth turned up a little as he gave Jesse a wink.

"Well, that didn't take long," Will said in a low voice. "Looks like he's about to open for business. And did you smell that when he opened the door?"

Jesse grimaced. "I'm sorry, but all I can smell is body odor. I really need a shower."

"You sound like my little brother," Will chuckled. "I'm talking about the trailer—I'm pretty sure I smelled pot. Probably just from sampling his own product."

"Do you think he's warehousing it in the trailer?"

"Not likely. He wouldn't want to get caught with a big stash in his living quarters. No deniability if somebody finds it. No, he's got his inventory hidden somewhere in that back lot. Keep a close eye on him when he comes back out."

For the next fifteen minutes, Will played with his phone while Officer Marquez stared at the area on the other side of the fence. He mentally searched every inch, trying to guess where Perez might be hiding his product. When the door to the trailer swung open, Will dropped his phone between his legs and turned his head back to the listening position.

Jesse lowered his chin and watched under his brow as Perez made his way to a rusted-out van body near the fence. After looking over both shoulders, he unlocked the side door of the vehicle and opened it. Ronny removed two shoebox sized parcels wrapped in plastic. As he slipped them into a black duffle bag, Jesse was able to get a quick glimpse.

The young officer had a look of excitement in his eyes as Perez headed toward the gate. As soon as the suspect cleared the lot, Jesse exploded.

"I saw it!"

"Saw what?" Will asked. "I couldn't see anything from this angle."

"He took two packages out of that old van." Jesse was breathing heavy. "I saw it on one of them!"

"Saw what?"

"*The mark*," Jesse blurted out. "One of the packages had the mark of the Green Legion!"

"I guess that settles it." Will punched a message into his phone and hit send. "We'll do the paperwork later. Right now, I need to have a talk with somebody."

Chapter 16

The music drifting overhead in Dugan's Pub mixed with the buzz of conversations and laughter. James took his usual seat at the end of the bar while the after-work crowd continued to filter in. As soon as his butt hit the stool, he was greeted by Donny's smiling face.

"You look wore out, little brother." The big man winked and grinned through his bushy red beard. "Missy keep you up late last night?"

"I wish," James replied shaking his head. "I was with Will."

Donny laid a bar napkin in front of James. "Well, that sounds like a lot less fun. I'm guessin' you need a drink."

"You guessed right." James eyed the rows of colorful bottles lining the shelves behind the bar. "I'll just take a beer tonight—none of the hard stuff. I've been in front of a computer all day, so I'd probably just go straight to sleep."

"Kept you out all night, did he?" Donny slipped a glass under the Smithwick's tap, drew a pint, and set it in front of his brother. "With all that runnin' around in the hills together, I'd a thought you two'd be tired of each other by now."

"Believe me, it wasn't my choice." James took a sip from his beer and slumped his shoulders. "He keeps pulling me back into this murder investigation."

"From what I hear, you had some pretty spot-on ideas. It don't surprise me he keeps pickin' your brain."

"I'm fine with him picking my brain," James sighed. "It's the *other* things I hate."

"Other things?" Donny raised one eyebrow. "What *other* things is Willy making you do?"

James looked around the bar before answering Donny in a low tone. "He made me pose as Jimmy Ray again last night."

"The drug buyer?" Donny leaned closer and lowered his voice as well. "What the hell was he thinking making you do that again? He got you arrested the last time he made you do a deal like that."

James took another drink and set the glass down. "It wasn't a drug sting this time. He wanted me to intimidate someone."

"You?" Donny snorted and choked back a laugh. "I'm sorry Jimmy, but—how do I put this tactfully—you don't really come off as a tough guy."

"I'm not, but I guess Jimmy Ray is supposed to be. The person he had me pressure was the other guy from the coffee shop—the partner of the man we found at the lake."

Donny shook his head. "I still don't get it. Willy can be plenty intimidating when he wants. What'd he need you for?"

"This man is the only person alive who knows what Jimmy Ray really looks like."

"Other than that Bernstein fella," Donny interjected.

"Okay, he's the only person alive, *outside of a jail cell,* that knows. Anyway, Will thought seeing me might scare the guy into giving him some information."

"Did he talk?"

James nodded. "Yeah, he talked. I'm not sure how, but it worked."

"What worked?" Margie spun James around on his stool, bending him down and hugging him tight enough to squeeze the air out of his lungs.

"Umm . . ." James couldn't get a word to come out of his mouth.

"Startin' that fire without a match," Donny blurted out. "Jimmy was just telling me how he done it."

"That's nice, but you boys can finish tellin' yer tales later." Margie turned to her oldest son. "Donny, table twelve needs another round a Black 'n Tans." With that, she grabbed a tray and began weaving between the tables, picking up empty glasses as she went.

James turned his stool back toward the bar. "Thanks for covering for me. I don't think Mom would be too happy if she found out about last night."

"Are you kidding?" Donny laughed as he grabbed a couple of pint glasses. "She'd bust a chair over Willy's head if she found out he put you in the line of fire again."

"She was pretty mad the last time, but can I confess something? You have to promise not to tell anyone, especially Will."

"Confessing to a bartender is like confessing to a priest—it goes no further than these ears." Donny began working on the layered beers as James spoke.

"I was scared last night, but I also got a little excited. When I saw the fear on that man's face, I have to admit it was kind of a rush." James looked his big brother directly in the eye. "For the first time in my life, I felt powerful—like I was in control."

"It's a great feeling Jimmy, but be careful. Power can be a potent drug. It makes smart men do stupid things."

"Don't worry." James managed a smile. "I'm not planning on starting my own cartel."

"Then you're putting this whole Jimmy Ray thing to bed, right?"

"I'd be happy if I never heard that name again." James propped his elbows on the bar and cradled his face in his upturned palms. "But I don't think Will feels the same way."

"Well, if he asks you to do it again, tell him *no*."

Donny placed the beers on a tray and set off to deliver them to the table as James muttered under his breath.

"I wish it was that easy."

The noise level in the bar continued to rise as the usual gang of rowdies gathered near the big TV. By now, James recognized the signs. This kind of activity signaled the start of some sporting event he didn't understand, being broadcast from somewhere he'd never been—it also meant Dugan's was about to get even louder and busier. As Donny returned with a tray full of empty glasses, James stood up and walked around the end of the bar.

"It looks like you're going to need some help." James picked up several more dirty glasses off the bar and stepped in front of the sink. "I can wash so you're free to fill orders."

Donny grinned and patted James on the back. "Seeing as how this is a family business, and you're family, I wouldn't mind the help."

James started in on the assortment of glasses piled up in the bar sink as Donny drew a couple more pitchers of beer and took off again. Over the last several months, James had spent enough time watching from his stool to know the routine—wash, double rinse, and rack. He smiled to himself as he worked. To him this wasn't a menial task, it's just something you do when you're family. For James, this kind of family was still a new concept, but one that made him happy.

"Are you actually whistling while you do that?" James looked up to find Missy leaning over the bar as she mounted the stool he had vacated. "I've never seen anybody so happy to have their hands in dishwater."

"I'm just helping Donny out with the rush." Missy ducked to one side as James smiled and flicked a little water in her direction. "It looks like there's a game about to start. I think it's rugby or something like that."

"Australian Rules Football." Missy motioned toward a particularly loud table. "I saw a bunch of Adelaide Crows jerseys over there when I came in."

"I've never heard of it." James looked at the big screen as the action on the field started. "How is it played?"

Missy shrugged her shoulders and smiled. "I don't think anybody really knows, but it's a hell of a lot of fun to watch. It's kinda like rugby, soccer and hockey all rolled into one . . . but with more blood."

"More blood than hockey?" James shuddered. "Why would anyone want to show that in here while people are eating?"

"Because it sells a lot of beer," Donny interjected as he returned with another tray full of empty glasses. "I found that satellite feed and figured I struck gold. When all the Aussie transplants in town heard we were showing the games, sales went up damn near ten percent. I had to double my Cooper's Ale order!"

"Well, aren't you just the marketing genius," Missy teased. "What'd you do, put one of those sign spinner guys on the corner?"

"Facebook 'n Twitter." Donny gave James a wink. "Josh McDaniel wrote an article on using social media to boost your business."

Missy looked back at James. "So now you're bookkeeper, dishwasher, and director of advertising? You're gonna own this place by Christmas."

"I wrote that article over a year and a half ago—long before I met Donny." James finished with the last glass and dried his hands on the towel draped over his shoulder. "And Mom asked me for help with the accounting software."

"Relax, Jimmy. I was just kidding." Missy patted the empty stool next to her as her boyfriend made his way back around the bar. "You're a little touchy today."

"Sorry." James sat down and put his arm around her. "I'm just tired."

"Because of that stuff with Will last night, right?" Missy laid her head on his shoulder. "I wish he'd just leave you alone."

"Me too." James felt his phone vibrate in his pocket. He pulled it out and looked at the screen. "Speak of the devil . . ."

James unlocked the screen and read the text message.

WILL: Where are you?
JAMES: At the bar.
WILL: Is Missy with you?
JAMES: Yes.
WILL: Keep her there. We need to talk.

Chapter 17

Will shoved the door to the crowded pub open and made a beeline for the bar, dodging tables and patrons as he went. The ratty looking detective hadn't bothered to stop at home and clean up after his stakeout. Approaching from behind, his sights were set on Missy. Donny looked up just in time to sound a warning.

"Incoming!" He pointed over Missy's shoulder. She and James spun their stools around in unison. Will's gritted teeth and furrowed brow spoke volumes. He stopped no more than foot in front of them and locked eyes with her.

"We need to talk . . . *now!*"

"Jesus, Willy, you smell like you been rollin' around in a barnyard!" Donny fanned the air with his bar towel. "Take it in the back before you run all the customers out!"

"Follow me." Will motioned to James as well. "Both of you!"

He turned, stormed through the kitchen door, and headed straight through to the storage room.

Missy put her arm around James as they trailed the huffing detective at a distance. "He doesn't look very happy."

James agreed. "I haven't seen him like this since the first time he showed up at my house."

Sometimes James still had nightmares about his first encounter with Will Dugan. The detective had showed up on his doorstep looking much the same way as he did tonight, demanding to know what James was trying to swindle from his mother. Since that time, Will had accepted James into the family and the two managed to work out most of their differences. Still, it worried James when he saw his brother like this.

"Any clue what the problem is?"

Missy had a worried look. "I have a pretty good idea."

When the pair came through the door, they found Will pacing back and forth, one hand on his hip and the other pushing his greasy hair out of his face. He stopped and stared straight at Missy. His voice came out in a low growl.

"Who the hell is Walter Franklin?"

"My Uncle Walt." Missy hung her head. "He's my dad's older brother."

"When were you gonna tell me?"

"Tell you what? That she has an uncle?" James pulled Missy closer.

"That he's a member of the Green Legion." Will's attention stayed locked on Missy. "And the kid that got busted transporting last year—one of your cousins?"

"Not a cousin." Missy looked up and bit her lower lip. "It was Jacob—my little brother."

James looked shocked. "Your *brother* is a member of the Green Legion?"

"How about you," Will barked. "Are you in the family business too?"

"No! And Jake's not either!" Missy pulled away from James and got right up in Will's face. "Uncle Walt talked him into making one delivery . . . *one!* He was so nervous he got caught the only time he did it."

Will crossed his arms and stood toe-to-toe with Missy. "Where is he now?"

"In jail. Uncle Walt just abandoned him there." She turned back toward James. "I've got to tell you something, Jimmy. I lied about my car—it didn't really break down. I sold it so I could hire an attorney for Jake. That's why I have to walk or take the bus everywhere I go."

"Why didn't you tell me?"

"It happened before we met—over a year ago. I didn't tell you because I didn't think you'd keep going out with me if you knew about all the crap with my family."

James took her in his arms and hugged her before kissing her on the top of her head. "You can have my Mom's Buick. I'll drive Nigel."

"Then *you'll* be the one taking the bus." She managed a little smile, but James could see the tears starting to form.

"I think I'm gonna puke." Will rolled his eyes and leaned against the wall. "I hate to break this up, but I need some answers. Why didn't you tell me you had an uncle who's a Legion member when all this shit started? You could have saved me a lot of time."

"Because he told me he's done with those guys." Missy dropped into a chair. "He said when Jake got busted it was the last straw—it put him out of business."

Will pulled another chair over and sat down directly in front of her. "And you bought that? You can't tell me losing *one* shipment put him out of the game. Legion members are growers, not middle men. Unless somebody took out his plants, he'd still have product."

"All I know is what he told me." Missy rubbed her nose as she shifted back in her chair to put some distance between them. "I tried to get him to help Jake, but all he did was complain about how legalization was ruining everything and how it was killing the market."

"Gee, I feel *sooo* sorry for him," Will sneered.

"Just leave her alone." James sat down next to her and put his arm around her. "You're treating her like *she's* involved in this."

"How do I know she isn't?" Will stood up, towering over Missy.

James stood as well and stepped in front of her. Facing the detective, he clenched his jaw. "She told you she's not . . . and that's good enough for me."

Will backed up a step, hitting the chair behind him. "Put 'em back in her purse, Jimmy. I know she's not a drug dealer."

"Then why are you treating her like she is?"

Will dropped back into his chair. "We found out Perez is getting at least part of his inventory from someone in the Legion."

"And you think it's her uncle?"

"I don't know—maybe, maybe not." Will sighed and rubbed the back of his neck. "But it's the only name I've got to go on."

"I admit I knew he'd been growing pot for years, but that doesn't make him a killer," Missy protested.

Will threw up his hands. "I'm just following the evidence. Dino was working for Ronny Perez when he turned up dead in a pile of bodies in Legion territory, and Perez is selling pot with the Legion's mark all over it. That and the mark over the entrance to the mine tells me the Legion is responsible for the homicides. Walter Franklin is the only member's name I have right now."

"Let's slow down and think this through, okay?" James sat back down. He leaned forward and spoke in a calm tone. "Whether her uncle is still growing marijuana or not isn't the issue here. You don't even know who Perez is buying it from, right? Don't you need to know that before you start pointing fingers?"

Will nodded. "That's the next piece of the puzzle."

"Okay." James settled back in his chair. "Then that's what we need to work on."

"We?" Missy grabbed his arm. "You're not getting in the middle of this again!"

"I'm already in the middle of it." James looked at Will. "Are we going to do the same thing we did with Mr. Bennett?"

Will shook his head. "I've been thinking about that, Jimmy. I know I said I was gonna use you when I questioned Ronny, but this guy's different . . . way worse than Bam-Bam. I can't put you in that kind of danger."

"But you need me—you need Jimmy Ray."

"This guy doesn't even know what Jimmy Ray looks like." Will stood up and started pacing again. "I can get another undercover to do it."

"How are you going to explain that to your partner? You're not supposed know anything about Jimmy Ray, so you wouldn't be able to guarantee Perez has never met him before." James crossed his arms and leaned back. "You'd have to admit you know Jimmy Ray isn't a real person."

"Yeah, that wouldn't work." Will scratched his head. "I guess I could just go in as Willy-D with the other cop playing the muscle."

"What if Bennett's already told Perez about our visit last night? If he says anything about Jimmy Ray, you'd have to explain to the other officer why Willy-D's been seen with him."

"What the *hell* are you doing?" Missy jumped up, grabbed James by the shoulders, and shook him. "He's letting you out of this shit and you're talking yourself right back in!"

"I'm doing it for you." James took her hands. "The only way to clear your family is to find out who's *really* responsible for those murders."

"You know what?" Missy threw her arms around his neck and began to cry. "I don't give a *shit* about those people anymore. I'll rat every one of them out if I have to. They're not my family now. *You're* my family!"

James pulled her into a tight embrace as she collapsed onto his lap. He gently rubbed her back. Missy buried her face in his shoulder and wept. Will stood silently watching for a few moments before turning away. He leaned forward, placing a hand on the wall and hanging his head.

"That's it . . . I can't ask you to do this." He slowly turned back around. "We've got enough to get a warrant now. We'll just have to keep him under surveillance until he makes another buy."

"You're not asking me to do this." James helped Missy back onto her chair and stood up. "I'm volunteering."

Will put a hand on his brother's shoulder. "Are you sure? Perez is dangerous and he's gonna be a lot harder to break."

James nodded. "It's the fastest way. More people could die while you're sitting around waiting for Perez to do something."

Will leaned his back against the wall and sighed. "Alright then, I guess it's time for Jimmy Ray to pay Ronny Perez a visit."

Chapter 18

Will sat behind the wheel of the dirty brown Crown Victoria, his face illuminated by the dashboard lights.

"Are you sure you're up to this, Jimmy? I wouldn't blame you if you backed out."

"For the last time, I'm *not* backing out." James fidgeted and picked at his fingernails.

Will swallowed the last bit of water out of a plastic bottle and tossed it in the back seat. "Alright, then let's go over it one more time."

"We don't need to go through it again. I've got it."

"Okay, then repeat it back to me." Will drummed his fingers on the steering wheel as he looked across the street at the front of the body shop. "We've only got one chance to get this right. If we lose him, he'll be packed up and gone by the time I can make it back out here with a warrant."

"Fine," James sighed. "I'm supposed to stay out of sight until you signal me. I need to keep a close eye on his body language—he may have hidden weapons. We want him to think the Legion killed one of our people as well, so . . ."

Will cut him off. "So, what's the number one rule?"

"Don't threaten his family like I did with Bennett—we need him on our side."

Will nodded. "Right, we want Perez to think we're on the same team."

"I know, Will. You've been beating me over the head with this for the last hour!" James scowled as he unbuckled his seatbelt. "Can we just get this over with?"

"There it is!" Will grinned and slapped James on the leg. "Now you're gettin' that pissed off look."

"You did all that on purpose just to provoke me?" James shook his head and looked away. "I can't believe you sometimes."

"You look more intimidating when you're mad—and you need all the help you can get."

James turned back toward his brother. "Don't you think it's funny that you're the only person who can make me angry?"

"I think it's hilarious." Will smiled. "It means I'm in your head."

"I don't think there's enough room in there for both you *and* Josh." James opened his door and stepped out of the car. "Let's just do this so I can go home."

Will turned the ignition off and met his brother in front of the car. "I'm gonna try to do this without you if I can, so stay out of sight unless I say otherwise. Keep your eyes peeled, and if things go south . . . run like hell."

James nodded and the two set off across the street. They approached the gate to the back lot using the shadow of the building's awning to shield them from the glow of a dim street light. Will pointed at the open padlock hanging from a short piece of chain and smiled.

"Looks like Ronny's open for business," Will whispered, sliding the gate to the side just enough to pass.

He peered through the opening and surveyed the area before slipping into the yard. The detective kept one hand on the gun tucked into the small of his back as he inched forward. Looking around the corner, he could see a silhouette cast on the curtains of the trailer. One person appeared to be moving around inside. He watched for a few moments to make sure the man was alone.

James whispered over Will's shoulder. "Are you just going up there and knock on the door?"

"Only if I want to get shot." Will pulled a phone out of his back pocket and held it up. "Unregistered phone. I twisted a few arms and came up with his burner number and the code word Ronny gives his customers. I sent him a text earlier to set up a buy. Once we're in position, I'll tell him I'm here. When he comes out, we can catch him off guard."

"Won't that scare him? He might shoot you anyway."

Will drew his weapon and held it up. "He won't get the chance."

James looked confused. "If you point a gun at him, isn't that counterproductive? I thought we were supposed to get him on our side."

"First I have to get his undivided attention," Will replied. "And if I do need your help, try not to use any big words like *counterproductive* with Perez. Keep it down to two or three syllables. He's smarter than Bam-Bam, but not *that* smart."

Will typed a message into the phone, and then motioned for James to follow him. They moved across the lot, trying as best they could to remain silent. The gravel crunching under their feet made the task difficult. James looked down at the ground with every step, as if it would somehow silence their approach.

When they reached the front of the trailer, Will held up his hand in a stop motion. He pointed at James and then to the ground, letting him know to stay put. He held up the phone and hit SEND before putting it back in his pocket and slipping around the corner of the trailer. He crouched under the window next to the door and waited. A few seconds later, the synthesized sound of a rooster crowing came from inside the trailer.

Message delivered, James thought as his stomach tightened. *Here we go.*

The dull thumping of footsteps could be heard as a shadow moved across the window again and stopped in front of the door. The click of the latch pierced the silence. Will pressed his body against the side of the trailer and raised his gun as the door swung open and Ronny Perez stepped out.

"Hands where I can see 'em!" Will stood up and stepped away from the trailer, his weapon aimed at the side of Ronny's head.

"What the . . ." Perez spun around and spread his arms. "You a fuckin' cop?"

"Do I *look* like a cop?" Will pointed at the man's right leg. "Lose the piece in your boot, Ronny—and the knife."

Perez slowly reached down and slipped a small .25 caliber semi-automatic out of an ankle holster and tossed it on the ground next to Will. He did the same with the lock-blade knife tucked into the top of his boot before straightening up.

"If you ain't a cop, then who the hell are you? I got people comin' any second. They walk through that gate and see you pointin' a gun at me, you're a dead man."

Will relaxed his stance, but kept the gun aimed at Perez. "I'm Willy-D, and I'm the one that sent you that message."

"You're Willy-D?" Perez took a step back and raised his hands a little higher. "Bam-Bam called me last night—drunk off his ass. Said he got a visit from you and your boss."

Will grinned. "Yeah, Bam-Bam's still a little broke up over his partner. He's also kinda worried he might end up in the same hole, seeing as how he was also working for you when Dino got it."

"Hey, if you're thinkin' I took Dino out you're dead wrong!" Perez protested. "I lost a shitload of cash when he didn't come back with the . . . parts . . . for one of the cars."

"Don't you mean the weed?" Will motioned toward the old van with his head. "And no, I don't think you killed Dino. I'm pretty sure it was somebody in the Legion."

Perez looked puzzled. "If you're so damn sure it was the Green Legion, then what the hell do you want from me?"

"My boss wants to know who you're buying from up there."

Perez shook his head. "I don't know what the hell you're talkin' about."

"Don't try that playing stupid shit on me." Will stepped sideways in the direction of the van Jesse had seen Perez access earlier. "How about we take a little look in your warehouse? Let's see whose mark we find on your inventory."

Perez held one hand up higher and moved in the same direction. "We don't need to go there. Why should I tell you who I'm dealin' with?"

"Because we're on the same side here, Ronny. The bodies are starting to pile up, and we both wanna know who's been killing off our people."

Perez pointed a finger at the gun in Will's hand. "If we're on the same side, why are you pointin' *that* thing at me?"

"Just trying to stay alive until we reach an understanding," Will replied. "Are we there yet?"

"Yeah, we're there." Perez slowly lowered his hands.

"Much better." Will lowered the gun, but kept a firm grip on it. "Now let's talk about our mutual problem. Who was Dino supposed to meet when he disappeared?"

"New supplier." Perez kept his eyes on the gun at Will's side. "My regular guy up an' disappeared. Haven't heard from him in a coupla months."

"This new guy have a name?"

"Calls himself El Toro. Fat white guy—wears a black, wide brimmed cowboy hat—bull rider style. Real piece a work."

"So . . ." Will paused and took a breath. "Your contact drops off the face of the earth and you get a new supplier right away—sounds a little convenient. How'd you find this guy?"

"I didn't find him, he found me. Called me up one day and said if I wanted to keep doin' business with the Legion, I had to deal with him now." Perez pointed at the phone sticking out of his front pocket. "I got a number if you want it."

Will nodded. "Damn right I want it."

Perez reached for the phone, then suddenly dropped his shoulder and lunged forward. He caught Will off guard, plowing into his chest. The detective tried to keep his balance, but it was too late. Perez had one arm wrapped around his torso, lifting him off his feet and driving him to the ground. His other hand caught the wrist of Will's gun hand. Stunned, James watched from the darkness as the two men tumbled around, fighting for control of the weapon.

Don't just stand there! Josh screamed in James' head. *DO SOMETHING!*

As Will struggled with the man on top of him, something caught James' eye. Ronny's small pistol still lay in the gravel where it had been discarded. James sprang from the shadows and made a beeline for the gun. In one smooth motion, he scooped it up, racked the slide to chamber a round, and aimed it at the back of Ronny's head.

"Get off him!" James growled with authority.

Perez rolled onto his back, eyes bulging as he stared down the barrel of his own gun. Will scrambled to his feet and stood next to James. He smiled as he dusted himself off and tucked his gun back in its place.

"I don't think you two have been properly introduced." Will put a hand on James' shoulder. "Ronny Perez, I'd like you to meet Jimmy Ray."

"Son of a . . ." Perez sat up and held his arms out wide with his palms up. "I'm unarmed, man. I didn't know . . ."

James pushed the gun close to Ronny's face. "I don't care what you didn't know. That was a stupid move." He glanced sideways at Will. "I thought you said this guy was smart."

Will shrugged his shoulders. "I guess I was wrong."

James lowered the gun, but kept his finger in the trigger loop. "Did you not hear Willy-D say we're on the same side?"

Ronny struggled to his feet. "Sorry man, but with all the people dyin' and disappearin' lately . . . I don't wanna be next."

"Then what else can you tell me about this *El Toro* you said contacted you?"

"Like I told him," Perez motioned toward the phone in his pocket again. "All I got is his number."

"Give the phone to Willy-D." James raised the gun again as Perez reached for his pocket. "No tricks this time."

Ronny carefully pulled the phone out and tossed it to Will. The detective caught it and slipped it into his pocket before bending down to retrieve the knife at his feet.

"I think we'll keep the gun," Will quipped as he tossed the knife through the open door of the trailer. "But I wouldn't want to leave you without *any* protection. This is a pretty rough neighborhood—you never know who might show up."

Chapter 19

Will turned the old Crown Victoria onto Central Avenue and headed south toward downtown. He couldn't stop glancing over at his brother in the passenger seat.

"You shocked the hell outta me back there, Jimmy."

"I kind of shocked myself too." James stared out the window into the darkness. "But I couldn't just stand there and watch. Perez was trying to kill you."

"He wasn't gonna kill me. I was just about to flip him over and pin his ass."

"I'm sorry." James lowered his head. "I know you told me to run if anything went wrong, but when I saw him on top of you, I just reacted."

"Cheer up, Bro. I'm not mad at you, I'm just surprised." Will reached over and punched him in the shoulder. "Where the hell did that Clint Eastwood move come from? When I handed you my gun a couple weeks ago, you were so freaked out you just about dropped it in the water."

"Yeah, that made me really nervous." James lifted his head and looked at Will. "I'd never touched a gun before. I didn't know what to do with it. When I got home, I watched a bunch of videos online so I could learn how to handle one safely."

"Videos?" Will scoffed and shook his head. "You can't learn how to handle a gun by watching videos!"

"Missy said the same thing." James managed a little smile. "She took me to an indoor range and taught me how to shoot. We rented a few different guns so I could get comfortable with them. The semi-autos were nice, but I think I prefer a revolver."

"One lesson from Annie Oakley and you're ready to make that call?" Will laughed. "You have no clue what you're talking about. Semi-autos have a higher capacity and a faster reload time. I can have a fifteen-round magazine swapped on my forty-five before you get one bullet out of your pocket."

"I've done some research, and I've been back to the range a couple of times—with a real instructor. Revolvers may have a lower capacity, but they're much more reliable. If a round doesn't fire, you can just keep pulling the trigger and it moves on to the next cylinder." James demonstrated with his hands as he talked. "If you have a misfire with an auto, or a cartridge stovepipes—you know, fails to load or eject and jams in the slide—then you have to clear it manually. That takes time and you end up moving your weapon off the target."

"I know what a stovepipe is, Jimmy." Will shook his head. "I still say the more lead you can get downrange, the better."

"You used a revolver when we talked to Bennett, and tonight too," James pointed out.

"That was a throw-away gun. I can't use my service weapon when I'm posing as Willy-D. That's just a little five round .38 Special—good for close-up work, but not much more." He held up his hand. "I use it when I need something I can hide in my palm."

"Missy calls that a purse gun."

"It's a *pocket* gun," Will sneered.

James laughed. "You don't have to get so touchy about it. I still have to say I prefer the reliability of a revolver."

Will grimaced. "Please tell me you haven't gone cowboy and bought yourself a six-shooter."

James shook his head. "I haven't bought anything. I just figured if I was going to be around guns now, I should know how to handle one."

"Well, you handled it pretty well back there with Perez." Will grinned and brought the car to a stop at a red light. "You really convinced him you knew what you were doing."

"We got the phone and nobody got hurt. I guess that's all that really matters."

Will accelerated again as the light turned green. "I would have got that number out of him eventually, but your move did speed up the process. Now we have his supplier's name, a description, and his contact info."

A worried look came over James' face. "Does the description fit Missy's uncle?"

Will shrugged his shoulders. "I don't know. I haven't been back to the precinct since I heard his name. I have no idea what he looks like."

"Maybe I should call her. She can tell us if it's him." James reached for his phone.

Will shook his head. "Hold off on that, Bro. No point in getting her stirred up again if this El Toro guy doesn't turn out to be her uncle."

James put the phone back down. "Are you worried she'll call and tip him off if the description fits?"

"After the way he screwed her brother?" Will laughed. "I'm more worried she'd go up there and take the son-of-a-bitch out before the law can get to him."

James' smile returned. "I watched her shoot a four-inch group at twenty-five yards. Uncle Walt wouldn't stand a chance."

Will nodded in agreement. "I think the best move now is to let Miller know what we've got, and then give Yazzi a call. This El Toro character is up in his territory. He might have a line on him already."

"What about Perez?" James pointed at the glove compartment. "Isn't that gun we took a parole violation? Are you just going to let him go?"

"I don't think it's a good idea to tell anybody about that gun, Jimmy. It's got your prints all over it now, and if it turns up as evidence against Perez, he'll know I'm a cop. Once word gets around, my Willy-D cover would be history. The drugs are enough to put him away again. I'll call Carl after I drop you off. He can get the warrant started and send the cavalry out to round up Ronny." Will picked up the dealer's phone off the dash. "The next thing I need to do is get this thing to the techs so they can unlock it."

"Do you mind if I give it a try?"

"Go for it." Will handed the phone over. "My prints are all over it now, so it's not like we're gonna get a clear set of Ronny's off it anyway. I'll clean it when you're done playing with it. I can just say the phone got wiped off when I put it in my pocket."

James took the phone and looked it over. He swiped his finger across the screen and then poked at it several times. Less than a minute later, he held it up. Will's jaw dropped when he saw the phone's contact list open.

"How the hell did you do that?"

"It was easy." James shrugged his shoulders. "First I tried swiping a common pattern in to see if the phone would give me an error. It didn't do anything, so that meant Perez must have used a number code instead of a pattern to lock it. I hit 1-3-9-7, the four numbers on the corners of the keypad going clockwise, and it opened right up."

Will shook his head. "I guess I gave Perez too much credit. He *is* just as stupid as Bam-Bam."

"He's got a bunch of numbers in here. Bam-Bam and Dino are both listed." James scrolled through the contacts. "Look at these names! Square Wheels, Maddmaxx, Long John . . . doesn't anybody in this business have a normal name?"

"Not that they want advertised," Will replied. "You see a number for somebody named El Toro?"

"Yup, right here." James held the phone up. "It's a 9-2-8 area code."

"That puts it up north. I'm sure the number's gonna come back as unregistered, but we might be able to track the location." Will thought for a moment. "I've just got to figure out how I can tie the phone back to Perez so we can get the order. That's not gonna be easy without fingerprints. I can't use you as a corroborating witness, so it'll just be my word against his."

"What about the battery?" James turned the phone over. "If he's played with the battery or the SIM card, he could have left prints or DNA on the inside."

"You're a damn genius!" Will grinned and punched his brother in the shoulder again.

James winced. "Would you stop doing that? It hurts!"

"Oh, come on." Will laughed and punched him one more time. "Toughen up! You're Jimmy Ray! Gun totin', badass drug dealer!"

"No, I'm James McCarthy—tired, stressed-out writer." He handed the phone back and rubbed his shoulder. "Can I go home now?"

"All right, I'll drop you off at the pub so you can get your car."

"I gave the Buick to Missy, remember?" James slumped in the seat. "You can just drop me at my house."

"No problem." Will rubbed the phone around on the leg of his jeans to remove James' fingerprints before setting it back on the dashboard. "I need to swing by the office anyway and log this thing into evidence."

They continued down Central Avenue for a couple more miles. James sat silently chewing on his fingernails and watching the lights of the city go by.

Will turned the car into the neighborhood and stopped at the curb in front of the house. He noticed Rose's Buick sitting in the driveway and was quick to point it out.

"I thought you said Missy had your mom's car."

"She does." James opened the door and slid out of the seat. "I wonder what she's doing here."

"Probably just making sure I brought you home in one piece." Will leaned over and opened the glove compartment. "Hold up a second, Jimmy." He grabbed Ronny's pistol and held the butt of the gun out toward James. "Take this and stash it somewhere. I don't want to get caught carrying it around the precinct after I sign the car back into the motor pool."

James took the gun in his hand and looked it over. He pressed a button on the side with his thumb and the magazine dropped out into his free hand. After clearing the chamber, he released the slide, reloaded the ejected round in the magazine, and slipped it back into the bottom of the grip with a loud click. He engaged the safety before tucking it into his back pocket.

Will laughed and shook his head as he waved. "See ya later, Dirty Harry . . ."

Chapter 20

Before James had a chance to close the front door, Missy already had her arms wrapped around him. She squeezed him like a boa constrictor.

"I'm *so* glad you're okay! This undercover stuff is getting out of hand. Will has *got* to stop making you play Jimmy Ray."

James returned the hug. "I volunteered, remember?"

"And I still don't get why you did it. I told you I don't care about those people anymore. My dad's abusive, my mom's an alcoholic, and my uncle's a drug dealer."

"Like it or not, you don't get to choose your family."

"You did." Missy looked up and shook her head. "Besides, you have *no* clue what kind of people you're dealing with now."

"I have a pretty good idea." James pulled the small semi-automatic pistol out of his pocket as he pushed the door closed with his foot. "Thanks for showing me how to use one of these. It came in handy tonight."

Missy pushed him away and stepped back, looking at the weapon in his hand. "You bought a *gun?* You shouldn't have done that without talking to me first!"

James set the pistol down on the table with his keys. "I didn't buy it. We took this one from Ronny Perez tonight. I almost had to use it on him."

Missy's eyes widened. "What do mean you almost had to use it?"

He led her over to the couch and sat, pulling her down next to him. "Perez got the jump on Will tonight and they fought. I was afraid the guy was going to kill him, so I picked the gun up off the ground, aimed it at Perez, and told him to stop."

Missy balled up her fists. "I can't believe that son-of-bitch almost got you shot!"

"It's okay, Missy. Nobody ever pointed a gun at *me*." James took her hands and tried to calm her down. "Will told me to run if anything went wrong. I'm the one that chose to step in, so it's not his fault."

"It sure as hell *is* his fault!" Missy's hands remained clenched so tight her fingernails started to dig into her palms. "You shouldn't have been there in the first place!"

"But it's a good thing I was." James massaged her hands, finally getting her to relax her fingers. "Anyway, we got what we needed from him. We have a lead on who he's buying from now."

Missy pulled her hands back. "Is it Uncle Walt?"

James shrugged his shoulders. "I don't know. All we have is the guy's nickname and a general description."

"What does he look like?" Missy gritted her teeth. "If it's Uncle Walt, I'll hunt that bastard down and kill him myself!"

James smiled. "That's exactly what Will told me you'd do. That's why he doesn't want me to share the description with you."

"Come on, Jimmy, you know I'm gonna get it out of you eventually." Missy furrowed her brow. "You might as well just give it up now."

"How about we do it this way," James sighed. "You tell me what your uncle looks like, and we'll figure it out from there."

"Fine . . ." Missy crossed her arms and planted her feet on the floor. "He's about six feet tall, and weighed maybe a hundred and eighty pounds the last time I saw him. He usually has a beard. Oh, and he's bald, so he always wears a hat."

"A cowboy hat?"

"Are you kidding?" Missy rolled her eyes. "He wouldn't be caught dead in a cowboy hat. Uncle Walt says they look stupid if you're not a real cowboy. He always wears some dumb trucker cap."

James breathed a sigh of relief. "I don't think it's your uncle. He doesn't fit the description. Perez said the guy he deals with is fat and wears a black cowboy hat."

"Well, that narrows it down to a few thousand people."

"If we assume it's someone who lives up in the Bradshaws, that reduces the numbers."

"Okay, so maybe a few hundred, if he's from that area."

"Since it's probably not your uncle, I guess it would be okay to tell you the rest." James settled back into the couch. "The guy calls himself El Toro."

"The Bull?" Missy thought for a second. "Did he say how old the guy was?"

James shook his head. "No, he didn't say anything about age. Just that the hat he wore was bull-rider style, whatever that is."

"That's like the kind Charlie Daniels wears."

"Charlie who?"

Missy patted his leg. "We need to get you out of that pub once in awhile and into a country bar."

James just smiled. "Getting back on subject, I know you haven't been back up there in a long time, but can you think of *anyone* from the area who might fit that description?"

"That still sounds like a lot of the guys up there." Missy's eyes shifted from side to side as she searched her memory. "Most of the men in Mayer wear cowboy hats. If you add in Bumble Bee, Cleator and Crown King—I don't know, Jimmy."

"What about people who also have a connection to bull riding?" James questioned. "Or maybe someone who owns a bull."

"That's still a pretty good list. There's gotta be a couple dozen ranches in the area and rodeos are pretty popular."

"Any of those people a little . . . um . . . shady?"

"A lot of them are, but now that you mention it," Missy paused and took a breath. "My cousin Ben—"

"You have a cousin named Ben Franklin?" James laughed out loud.

"Ben Weber," she said shaking her head. "He's not *really* my cousin. He lived with Uncle Walt and Aunt Minnie for a couple years after his parents died. I guess he'd be about forty now."

"Is he a bull rider?"

"Oh, God no," Missy chuckled. "He wanted to be one, but he didn't have the skill or the build for it—short, fat guy with a Napoleon complex."

"What makes you think it might be him?"

"He may not have been a bull rider," she explained, "but he dressed like one. He wore the big hat, cowboy boots, and a belt buckle the size of his head. Ben also looked up to Uncle Walt big-time. He followed him around like a damn puppy, even after he moved out."

"Do you think he looked up to him enough to follow him into the drug business?"

Missy nodded. "It wouldn't surprise me. The little shit also had a mean streak a mile wide."

James barely took a breath between questions. "Do you know if he still lives in the area?"

"I'm not sure." She thought for a moment. "I know he bought some property somewhere off Table

Mesa north of New River a few years ago, but I don't think he ever lived there. He was going to build some kind of bunker—you know, 'prepper' stuff."

"Off Table Mesa?" James stood up and walked over to his desk. He pulled a file out of the lower drawer and returned to the couch. "These are copies of the maps we used when we found the mine."

He spread the contents of the folder out on the coffee table, piecing the individual pages together into one large map. "Can you show me where his property was?"

"I'm not a hundred percent sure, but I think it was right in this area." Missy pointed to a spot west of I-17, just before a dirt road crossed the Agua Fria River. "I know it was somewhere east of the riverbed."

James put his finger on the map and traced Table Mesa Road as it crossed the river and continued west. He followed the track from one page to the next, stopping where the road turned south and dead-ended on the third sheet. Backtracking one page, he found a fork in the road that went farther west. The road jumped one more map before passing a spot marked with a red ring around it. One word was written under the crimson circle—**Bodies**!

Missy and James both looked up slowly. When their eyes met, she was the first to speak.

"That *can't* be a coincidence, right?"

James shook his head. "The odds are pretty slim. If you have the location of the property correct, it's not looking good for your cousin."

"I guess we have to let Will know," she sighed. "He's never gonna let me hear the end of this."

"Let's not get ahead of ourselves," James replied. "We need to do a little more research first."

He took her hand and led her back to the desk. James pulled a dining room chair over for his girlfriend before sitting down in front of the computer.

"We can look at the zoning maps online and find any private parcels of land in that area. Once we have parcel numbers, we can go to the County Recorder's site and do title searches on them."

Missy looked surprised. "You can do that?"

"It's all a matter of public record." James began navigating his way through the pages of information. "You just have to know where to look. The Yavapai County Recorder's Office has everything from 1974 to the present scanned and indexed. You can search it all on the web now."

Missy smiled and rubbed his arm. "How did you get so smart?"

"I didn't have a life to distract me, remember?" James pointed at the monitor. "Okay, here's the property map of that area. Which plot do you think belongs to Ben?"

Missy studied the screen before pointing out a spot. "It should be one of these over here. I know it was supposed to be right next to the riverbed."

James made a list of the parcel numbers before switching to another tab in the browser. He typed in his search information and waited for the results to load. A few seconds later, the screen filled with rows of text.

"Here we go." James began scrolling through the lines of information. "I narrowed the search down to the last ten years. We can go back farther if we don't find anything."

"Stop!" Missy slapped his leg and pointed at the bottom of the screen. "There it is—a deed recorded for Benjamin J. Weber."

James clicked on the link to display the document. "Are you positive this is your cousin?"

"Give me that." She grabbed the mouse out of James' hand and scrolled to the bottom of the document. "That's his signature. I saw it on enough bounced checks. I'd recognize it anywhere."

"I guess that settles it." James leaned back in the chair and dug his phone out of his pocket. "Do you want to make the call, or should I?"

Chapter 21

Carl Stiverson was already at his desk and hard at work by the time Will managed to drag himself into the squad room.

"Well, look at you." Carl whistled at his partner. "All showered and shaved . . . even combed your hair!"

Will dropped his messenger bag by his desk and flopped down into the chair. "Don't give me any crap, Carl, I'm not in the mood. I have a meeting with Miller and a couple of the guys from the taskforce this morning."

"Is Yazzi gonna be there?"

"God, I hope not," Will sighed. "But everything's pointing up to his neck of the woods, so . . ."

"So the odds ain't in your favor." Carl grinned and shook his head. "I'm telling you, Doogie, listen to the guy and keep an open mind."

"Yeah, I know." Will hit the power button on his computer and started unloading paperwork from his bag. He tossed the folders on top of the growing piles already occupying his desk. "I was up half the night writing this damn report. You get anywhere on the warrant for Ronny Perez? Jesse seeing him in possession of the pot should have been enough to push it through."

Carl nodded. "Sitting on the judge's desk waiting for a signature. Should have it back by lunchtime."

"Thanks." Will opened a folder and pulled out a few pages. "The sooner we get that piece of garbage off the street, the better."

"I still can't believe you went back out there last night without Marquez." Carl gave him a disgusted look. "You're never gonna get it through your thick skull. You can't keep going off on your own like that."

"Would you quit being such a mother hen? I told you I couldn't take Jesse when I confronted Perez—he's too clean-cut. That kid could *neve*r pass as a street-level dealer."

"Did you recruit some damn low-life thug again?"

Will nodded. "I took the same guy I had with me when I questioned Bennett."

"I still say you need to take another cop when you go off like that. How do you know you can trust this guy to have your back?"

"Believe me, Carl, I trust him like a brother." Will looked away from his partner. "And he proved himself last night. He stepped up when things got a little rough."

Carl spun his chair around. "Whadda you mean by *a little rough*?"

"I mean Perez tried to jump me, but we handled it," he replied, still avoiding eye contact. "By the way, don't be surprised if Ronny's a little bruised when they pick him up. We kinda rolled around in the gravel."

Will turned his chair and pulled his shirt up in the back, exposing the large black and blue mark where he hit the ground when Perez tackled him.

"Man, you're some piece of work." Carl shook his head. "You've been spending too much time on the streets. You're starting to think you're invincible—like you really *are* Willy-D."

"I do whatever it takes to get the job done." Will pulled his shirt back down and handed a couple of stapled pages across the aisle. "I got a name, a description, and a cell number for his supplier. I also ended up with Ronny's phone after our little wrestling match. We might be able to use the contact list and text history to breathe some new life into a few other cases we have floating around here."

"Lab techs have already have it?"

"Yup. They're pulling prints so we can have a solid connection to Perez, then they'll send us a dump of all the data."

Carl pointed at one of the pages. "Jesse told me about this Walter Franklin character. He said the way you reacted it looked like you might know something about the guy. Wanna fill me in?"

"You remember Missy Franklin? The woman that accidentally got mixed up in one of the vice sweeps we did a while back?"

"The little lady that tried to kick a field goal with your family jewels?" Carl laughed and nodded. "You bet I remember, and that was no accident. You know you did that to her on purpose."

"Yeah? Prove it." Will finally looked his partner in the eye. "Anyway, she's McCarthy's girlfriend now. Walter Franklin is her uncle."

"The same Walter Franklin Jesse was talking about?"

"That's the one," Will replied. "The kid that got busted that night was Missy's brother. According to her, the boy wasn't a member of the Green Legion, but the old man was."

Carl raised one eyebrow. "You thinking her uncle might be this El Toro guy Perez talked about?"

Will shook his head. "I don't think so. She says her uncle told her he was done with the Legion after losing that shipment. I don't know whether to believe that or not, but he doesn't fit the description anyway. McCarthy gave me another name to look into last night."

"You still keeping him in the loop?" Carl smiled and nodded. "Glad you're finally seeing the light about him. I don't usually like sharing too much information with civilians, but that boy's different—he's got one hell of a head on his shoulders."

"He's a freakin' genius," Will replied with a note of sarcasm. "He can also get Missy to spill her guts. She doesn't like to share with me. A bus could be headed straight for my ass and she wouldn't say a word."

"Can you blame her?" Carl laughed. "You stuffed her into a wagon with a bunch of sweaty hookers."

"For the last time, that wasn't my fault! She was just in the wrong place at the wrong time."

"Right . . ." Carl grinned and turned back to his desk. "Let's get back to the case, okay? What's the other name your brother got outta the girl?"

"Benjamin J. Weber." Will dug out a few more sheets and handed them across the aisle. "The guy lived with her uncle for a while after his parents were killed. He even dresses like a bull rider, so the El Toro name fits. I haven't pulled his record yet, but get this—he owns property in the Bradshaws along the same road that leads to the mine where we found the bodies."

Carl looked over the documents. "Nice piece of work using the title search to locate the property. You pull all this together last night?"

Will shook his head. "I wish I could take the credit, but that was all McCarthy. He sent that stuff to me, along with everything Missy told him about Weber. In fact, most of the information in that report . . . I just cut and pasted it right out of his e-mail."

Carl grinned. "I should have guessed. There's a bunch a big words in here."

"Very funny." Will reached across the aisle and snatched the papers back. "I need to see if this rodeo clown's got a RAP Sheet before I head over to my meeting at County."

Carl shook his finger at Will. "Don't be making fun of rodeo clowns. Those guys are some tough sons-a-bitches."

"How the hell would you know?" Will typed the name into his computer and looked at his partner. "You've never even been to a rodeo. You're afraid of the damn horses."

"I've seen rodeos on TV," Carl fired back. "And I am *not* afraid of horses. I just have a healthy respect for some heavy breathing hunk of meat coming at me like a freight-train."

Will grinned. "I'll bet suspects feel the same way every time you try to chase one of them down."

Carl shot him a dirty look. "Don't you have someplace else you're supposed to be?"

"I'm heading out as soon as Weber's record hits the printer."

Will walked to the end of the row of cubes and retrieved the still warm pages from the machine. He returned to his desk and stuffed them in his bag, along with several file folders from his cluttered desk.

"You driving over there?"

Will shouldered his bag. "It's only two blocks. Why would I drive?"

"There's another storm moving in." Carl held up his phone and pointed at the weather app. "Supposed to be a whopper today."

Will just waved it off. "I'll take my chances. A little water never hurt anybody."

"Suit yourself." Carl put the phone back on his desk and smiled. "Say hello to Nestor for me!"

Chapter 22

James sipped his third cup of coffee as he stared at the text on his computer. It seemed no amount of caffeine could get him to concentrate on his work this morning. After the events of the previous night, performing research on the latest advances in dishwasher technology failed to excite him. Instead, he found the pointer of his mouse being pulled toward another tab in his browser.

Don't do it, Jimmy. Josh shook a mental finger in James' face. *You need to stay on task or we'll never get this article done.*

James clicked the tab anyway, revealing a satellite map. "Something doesn't look right. I can't stop thinking about it."

Well you'd better, or Simon might stop thinking about giving us more work.

"He's not going to do that. I'm his biggest seller."

No, I'm his biggest seller, but if you don't start spending more time writing and less time playing cops and robbers, I won't be for long.

"Look at this." James zoomed in on Ben Weber's property. "See this spot on the east side of the lot?"

You do realize we both use the same eyes, right?

"The plants and rocks feel arranged—like somebody *tried* to make them look natural, but there's a definite pattern. It also looks like there's a pile of brush or something up against this embankment." James moved closer to the screen and squinted. "I wish I could see more detail."

Maybe you can hack a high-resolution military satellite. They do it on TV all the time.

"I'm not a hacker. I wouldn't even know where to start."

That's what's stopping you? Not the fact that you could end up in prison? You're starting to worry me, Jimmy.

"What if I drove out there, took a look around? You know, just casually drive by."

And just casually get shot?

"I can drive by slow. I don't have to stop. I mean . . . it's a public road, right? People drive by all the time."

I see two problems with your plan. First, you can't take the Buick on that road—you'd get it stuck and tear it up. Second, Missy has the Buick so you're without wheels anyway.

"I have Nigel. He's got four-wheel drive and a lot more ground clearance."

He's also got electrical problems and a ton of rust.

"Missy and I got the wiring sorted out—and it's just surface rust. He'll be fine"

Famous last words . . .

James got up and headed down the hall to the bedroom. Ten minutes later, he emerged wearing his boots, a faded pair of jeans and a tan T-shirt. He made a stop in the kitchen where he filled a canvas cooler with several water bottles from the refrigerator and a handful of energy bars. Grabbing his keys and sunglasses, he headed for the back door.

As he passed through the laundry room, he paused and stared at the cabinet above the dryer. After a moment of contemplation, he opened the cupboard door and reached to the back. When he pulled his hand out, it was no longer empty—it held the gun he and Will had taken from Ronny Perez.

What the hell do you think you're doing?

"I just feel like I should take it." James slipped the gun into the outside pocket of the bag. "It's better to have it and not need it, than to need it and not have it—right?"

If you think you need a gun, maybe you shouldn't be going up there in the first place!

James ignored the voice in his head and continued out to the detached garage. He hit the button on the wall, sending the garage door into motion. As the morning sunlight streamed in, he grabbed a hat off the workbench and tossed it on the passenger seat along with the cooler. He slid into the driver's side and stuck the key in the ignition.

A familiar cloud of black smoke filled the air as Nigel backfired once and then roared to life. Since the first time Missy started the engine in the closed garage, James had learned an important lesson—always open the big door before firing up the beast. He backed out of the garage, and after letting the smoke clear a little, hit the remote to close the door.

James felt strangely out of control as he guided the Land Rover down the narrow alley for the first time. Driving on the right-hand side of the vehicle was a new experience. When he pulled out onto the street, he wasn't quite sure of his lane position. Several times he caught himself drifting over the centerline into oncoming traffic. It took a few miles and several turns before he felt comfortable having the sidewalks and parked cars so close to him.

He swung by Dugan's to borrow Donny's GPS, and then made a quick stop at a gas station. As he approached the onramp to I-17, James took a deep breath and ventured onto the freeway. He stuck to the right-hand side, only changing lanes when absolutely necessary. This was partly due to the fear of hitting another car, but mostly because he didn't want to make the other drivers angry. Nigel seemed incapable of going over sixty miles per hour—even with the help of a stiff, monsoon tailwind.

He drove north past the edge of the city, his hair flying in all directions due to the open windows. The air conditioner was one thing he and Missy had not been able fix. James grabbed the hat off the seat next to him and pulled it over the haystack on his head. He continued past the exits for Anthem and New River, pulling off at Table Mesa Road.

James felt both nervous and excited at the same time as he slowed to a stop at the top of the ramp. He turned west and passed over the highway, following the road where it turned from blacktop to dirt and passed by a gravel pit. He checked the GPS suction-cupped to the windshield for directions as he approached a fork in the road. James followed the track to the left where the relatively smooth, graded surface gave way to a rutted, washboard road. The farther he traveled, the rougher it got, slowing his progress. As he approached Weber's property he slowed even more, eventually coming to a full stop.

Have you lost your mind? I thought you were only going to do a drive by.

"I just want to take a quick look. I don't see anybody around."

That doesn't mean they don't see you.

"I'll be careful."

James pulled off onto a flat spot across the road from the property and shut the engine off. He looked around one more time before getting out and walking toward the area he had identified in the satellite image. Several sets of tire tracks crisscrossed the lot, the majority of them leading to a pile of brush pushed up against a rocky ledge running along one edge of the property.

As James got closer, his suspicions were confirmed. He pulled back a few of the dried branches, exposing two tan metal doors secured with a large padlock. They appeared to be the doors of a shipping container that had been buried in the embankment. He replaced the branches and picked his way up the hill. James inspected the area above the doors. Even with the recent rains, he could tell that the ground had been disturbed and plants relocated in an area stretching from the edge to a line at least forty feet back.

"I *knew* it!" James smiled as he continued to look around. "I knew he had something hidden up here! He's got a huge box buried under right under our feet."

Okay, so you found the guy's bug-out shelter. That doesn't prove anything. Missy said he was a prepper.

"It's not a bug-out shelter. I don't see any exhaust vents or a way to get fresh air inside—this thing is sealed up tight. I'll bet it's where he stores his inventory."

Great. You've solved the big mystery. Now can we get the hell out of here before somebody sees you?

James slid back down the bank and headed toward the road. He climbed into the driver's seat and started Nigel up again. The usual puff of black smoke dissipated faster this time as the fresh gasoline made its way through the fuel system. He slipped the Rover into gear and pulled back onto the road, continuing west.

Where do you think you're going? You got what you came for, let's get out of here!

"I just want to go a little farther."

You've seen the maps. You know where this road goes.

"I want to see what else is around here. I won't go all the way up to the mine."

As James moved the car forward, the road dropped into the dry Agua Fria river bed. It followed the wide, flat bottom for a mile or so before turning and climbing back out on the western bank. He had to engage Nigel's untested four-wheel drive system to make it up the rocky slope. To his delight, it worked on the first try without missing a beat.

James stopped in a flat area on top and surveyed the furrowed double-track path ahead. It was obvious the road was no longer being maintained on this side of the river. Nevertheless, there were fresh tire tracks that had to have been made since the last rain a few days earlier. James kept the four-wheel drive engaged and crept forward.

I'll bet those tracks are from the Yavapai County guys processing the scene up at the mine.

"Maybe . . ." James stopped at a fork in the trail. "But according to the GPS, the mine is to the left at this junction. The freshest tracks are going the other way."

Please tell me that means we're going to the left.

James slowly let out the clutch and moved his other foot from the brake pedal to the gas as he cranked the steering wheel . . . to the right.

Chapter 23

Will stood in front of the mirror in the men's room on the third floor of the County Sherriff's office. He scowled as he ran a handful of paper towels over his wet hair.

"Dumbass! You should have listened to Carl and just drove the two damn blocks." He grabbed a couple more towels and tried to dry his rain-soaked shirt while he eyed his reflection. "And now I'm talking to myself. I gotta stop running around with Jimmy before I start answering."

He tossed the towels in the trashcan, flipped the top of his messenger bag open, and checked the contents. Even though it was damp on the outside, the rain from the sudden downpour had not made its way into the bag. He breathed a sigh of relief, closed it, and headed out the door.

When he reached the small meeting room, Will found several people already seated. Nestor Yazzi was on the far side of the table wearing his usual flat expression. He rose and reached across table, shook Will's hand without saying a word, then sat back down and folded his arms across his chest.

The young woman to Yazzi's left looked up long enough to flash a quick smile. She pushed her glasses up with her index finger, tucked her long, red hair behind her ear, and went back to shuffling the papers in front of her. The man to Nestor's right was still as a statue. Will watched him for a few seconds to see if the guy was even breathing.

"Grab a seat, Dugan." Sergeant Mike Miller sat at the head of the table poking at his laptop and fooling with the cords.

Will took a seat opposite Nestor and pulled out a handful of files. He dropped the wet messenger bag on the floor and shoved it under the table with his foot.

"We'll get started as soon as I can get this damn projector to work." Miller waved a hand in Nestor's direction. "Yazzi, go ahead and introduce your entourage."

Nestor tilted his head toward the man on his right. "Detective David Alexander, lead CSI for Yavapai County on this case." Nestor nodded toward Will. "Detective William Dugan, Phoenix PD."

The statue finally moved enough to reach out and shake Will's hand, then immediately sat back and assumed his previous position.

Nestor leaned his head in the other direction. "Dr. Sarah O'Donnell, Deputy Medical Examiner."

Will stood to shake her hand. When Sarah leaned forward and extended her arm, her tortoise-shell framed glasses slipped down the bridge of her nose. Will felt his stomach tighten when they made eye-contact. Their hands separated as he sat back down, but Will's gaze stayed locked on her green eyes.

"I'm also a forensic anthropologist." She smiled and pushed her glasses back up again. "Pleased to meet you."

"Not as pleased as I am," Will muttered. He felt his face flush as soon as the words came out of his mouth.

Nestor shook his head. "Still haven't learned to think before you speak."

Will shot him a dirty look just in time to see the corners of the deputy's mouth turn up. Nestor winked before straightening his expression again.

"Aw, fu . . . screw it!" Miller glanced in Sarah's direction as he shut the projector off and shoved it to one side. "I already e-mailed everything to you guys anyway. We don't need to rehash the old information. Dr. O'Donnell, go ahead and start. What's the body count up to?"

"So far we've at least partially reconstructed nine victims." Sarah glanced at Will with a coy smile. "Not including the body Detective Dugan initially found in Lake Pleasant."

"Just call me Will." He felt his face get warm again.

Miller rolled his eyes. "Get your tongue back in your head, Dugan." He turned back to Sarah. "Any details you want to share, Doctor O'Donnell? Got any IDs yet?"

She cleared her throat and looked down at her files. "No positive identifications yet, but we have determined that all of the victims are male. One has a three-inch, titanium plate on the left radius just above the wrist. Bone re-growth indicates the fracture is two to three years old. We recovered the serial number off the appliance and we've contacted the manufacturer for information on the patient implanted with the device."

Miller nodded. "It's a start. Benitez and Styles have been going through missing persons reports and requesting dental records on likely candidates—they send you anything yet?"

"We've received six files, but there haven't been any matches so far." She pulled a paper out and studied it for a few seconds. "We haven't finished reconstructing four of the bodies, so there's still a chance."

"I think they have a couple dozen files left to go through." Miller rubbed his temples. "How long before you finish putting these guys back together?"

"It could be several weeks—maybe months. We're down to using DNA to match the single teeth and smaller bone fragments to specific victims."

Will grinned. "Kinda like building a bunch of jigsaw puzzles with all the pieces dumped into one big pile."

Dr. O'Donnell wrinkled her nose. "A revolting image, but that would be a good analogy. The difference is we don't have the pictures on the boxes to use as a guide. We have no idea what any of these men looked like."

"Or how many puzzles you're dealing with," Will replied. "At least you know they're all men."

"So far . . ." Sarah looked over her glasses and smiled as she restacked her folders into a neat pile.

"Let me know when you make more progress." Miller made a note on a pad. "I'll pass the info on the busted arm to my guys. They can keep an eye out for it in their files."

"Already done," Nestor replied. "I forwarded the report on to Benitez this morning before we left Prescott."

"Looks like you guys are on the ball." Miller crossed the note off and turned to Detective Alexander. "Anything new to report from the crime scene?"

Alexander finally showed signs of life as he opened a folder on the table in front of him. "We've wrapped up our work at the scene of the mine. I still have three technicians in the field working in the creek bed south of the confluence with Rich Gulch, but I don't expect them to find much more."

"Anything interesting from the mine?" Miller asked. "Or just more pieces for Dr. O'Donnell to play with?"

"Twenty-eight complete bullets and thirty-seven additional fragments have been recovered from the mine. Twelve of the complete slugs appear to be nine millimeters, the rest are forty-five caliber. The lab has them now." He moved just enough to turn the page of the report. "We also found seventeen spent nine millimeter cartridges near the airshaft at the top of the hill. Oxidation and weathering indicate some were fired at different times. The ejector marks on all the casings match, so it's likely they were fired from the same weapon."

"No forty-five brass?" Will questioned.

"None."

"So you probably have at least two shooters." Will drummed on the table with his pen. "One guy with a semi-auto, the other with a revolver."

Alexander stared at Will. "How did you come to that conclusion, Detective?"

Will pointed toward the report Alexander had been reading from. "No ejected brass from the forty-five."

The detective scoffed. "He could have policed the area."

"One guy takes the time to clean up the scene, but leaves the other guy's brass?" Will shook his head. "Not likely."

"I agree with Dugan." Yazzi interjected.

Will looked at Nestor. "I'm thinking we might have a guy who likes cowboy guns."

Nestor nodded again. "It's a good bet."

"Nice catch, Dugan." Miller made another note. "What else have you got? I understand you went back up to Sunnyslope alone last night after you dropped off Officer Marquez."

"Yup." Will shuffled a few papers and pulled out a file. "I sent you a copy of the report this morning."

Miller scrolled through his inbox. "Got it. So, you managed to get the supplier's street name and a cell number? Good work."

"I can go one better than that." Will handed over a couple of pages. "I have a possible name to go with it now—Benjamin J. Weber. I just pulled his RAP sheet before I came over—haven't had a chance to go through it yet."

"Ben Weber." Nestor frowned. "Looks like a dime-store cowboy—acts like a punk."

"So, you know this guy?" Miller asked.

"Calls himself El Toro. We've crossed paths a few times."

Will slapped the table and grinned. "That's the name I got out of Perez! Any idea what kind of heat he packs?"

Nestor held up his index finger. "I'll give you one guess."

Will smiled "Oh, come on. It can't be that easy."

Nestor gave a single nod. "Chrome Peacemaker chambered in .45 Long-Colt."

"This guy sounds like a walking cliché." Miller leaned back in his chair. "But just because he's a drug dealer and a general jackass, that doesn't make him a killer."

"Oh, I have more. The guy owns property on the same road that leads to the mine." Will pulled another file out. He spread out the maps and title information James had sent him. "My brother managed to dig this stuff up last night."

Miller studied the pages. "This brother the same kid I met out at the lake?"

"Yeah, Jimmy." Will grinned. "He's a lot better with this Internet search stuff than me."

Nestor looked over the papers as well. "Stray Dog is a very smart man."

"Who's Stray Dog, another dealer?" Miller asked.

"No, Dugan's brother," Nestor replied. "His analysis led us to the mine."

Sarah smiled at Will. "Your brother's also an investigator?"

"No, he's a writer—kind of a geek, but he does come up with some pretty good theories."

Detective Alexander scowled at Will. "You had a civilian at *my* crime scene?"

"Without that civilian you wouldn't even *have* a crime scene," Will shot back.

Alexander started to lean forward, but Nestor put a hand on his shoulder. "Calm down. I was in charge, not Dugan. Stray Dog did nothing to compromise the scene. He was a great help."

"I'm not real thrilled about a civilian being this deep in the investigation either." Miller looked at Yazzi. "But I trust your judgment. Hell, we should probably go ahead and put him on the damn payroll, considering everything the kid's contributed to this case so far."

Will put his hand over his mouth and mumbled. "You have no idea . . ."

Chapter 24

James inched the old Land Rover forward along the rutted path. He found it difficult to think of it as a road. The surface seemed no better suited to travel than the surrounding desert. When he thought about the history of the area, he pictured something much different. James imagined rugged men in equally rugged trucks from the early twentieth century. He could see them loaded with ore from some mine deep in the mountains, kicking up the dust as they rolled past on its rough-graded surface.

The tracks he followed today were not made by mining machines of the past, but something more modern. In places where the rocks and gravel gave way to dirt and sand, James could make out at least two distinct tread patterns. Both vehicles had wider tires than Nigel. One set of tracks matched those he had seen around the storage container. As he advanced, Josh rattled around in his brain.

This is stupid. You know that, right?

"I just want to see what's over the next ridge." James kept the Rover moving forward, gaining elevation as he went. "I'll turn around when I get to the top."

Turn around where? This path is barely wide enough for one vehicle.

"If I can't find a spot on the ridge, I'll back down until I see someplace wide enough."

You can barely drive this thing going forward.

Nigel bounced back and forth as James guided him up the twisted path clinging to the side of the hill. Bushes overhanging the trail scraped against the side of the car, leaving marks in the faded paint—Will called it desert pin-striping. Halfway to the top, the right front tire dropped into a deep hole. The steering wheel jerked violently to one side. As the car rebounded, James' hand slipped off the wheel, hitting the shifter and knocking it out of gear. By the time he got his foot on the brake, Nigel managed to roll backward several feet leaving the right rear tire dangerously close to the edge of a steep drop off.

James stepped on the clutch and put the vehicle back in gear. He let the pedal out just enough to hold the Rover in place while he moved his other foot from the brake to the gas. He throttled the engine and let the clutch out the rest of the way, cranking the wheels to the left to miss the hole. Nigel lurched forward about ten feet and bounced off a large rock before the engine stalled.

Stomping a foot on the brake again, James managed to stop the Rover this time before it moved backward. He put it in neutral and turned the key to engage the starter, but nothing happened. He turned the ignition all the way off and tried again. Nigel still didn't make a sound.

Great . . . you killed it. What are you gonna to do now, genius?

"I don't think I can work on it at this angle, so I guess I'll have to let it coast back down the hill." James turned to look over his shoulder and eased his foot off the brake. "I just hope I can find a spot to get off the road."

Nigel rolled backward, picking up speed as he went. James did his best to stay off the brake and maintain momentum while still keeping control of the vehicle. Nigel bounced and pitched worse than on the way up. Before he reached the next big corner, James saw a flat spot between the bushes to the left of the trail—he turned the wheel and aimed for it. Nigel jumped out of the ruts and over the small embankment. James hit the brakes and skidded to a stop in a cloud of dust. He leaned over the steering wheel and breathed a sigh of relief as the air cleared.

After regaining his composure, he got out and lifted the hood. It didn't take but a few seconds to discover the problem. The rusty battery tray had collapsed on one corner. The battery now hung at an angle, secured only by the ground strap. The positive terminal was ripped out of the case and dangled from the end of its cable.

Must have been that last bump. Good luck fixing it.

"I'm afraid that isn't going to happen out here." James closed the hood and sat on the bumper. "Even if I could find a way to prop the battery back up, I can't fix the terminal."

So, what now?

James pulled his phone out of his pocket. "I have a weak signal, but I don't think I'll be able to get a tow truck to come out here anyway. Will's the only one I know with a Jeep and he's at work."

Looks like you're riding the 'Shoe-leather Express' outta here.

"I guess that's my only choice. It's about five or six miles back to that gravel pit. Maybe I can get help there. I should see if I can get a message out."

James typed a text to Will and hit send. The phone chewed on it for a few seconds and then returned its own message—Network Not Available.

At least you've got food and water. Better get a move on.

James walked around to the passenger door, grabbed his hat, and picked up the insulated bag off the floorboard where it had landed during the rough ride. He slung the strap over his shoulder and surveyed the surrounding desert as he donned his cap. Gray clouds covered the sky.

From his vantage point on the side of the hill he could see a large thunderhead dumping a heavy load of rain somewhere over the city, but the breeze coming down from the mountain felt warm and dry. He turned and looked back up the narrow track.

"It's not that far to the top and I might be able to get a better signal up there. I could hike that in less than ten minutes."

That's just an excuse. You still want to see what's on the other side of that ridge.

"It couldn't hurt to look around a little bit while I'm up there."

I'm not gonna to talk you out of this, am I?

James ignored his inner voice and headed up the hill. Even with the cloud cover blocking the late August sun, the heat continued to build. He made it to the top in a little more than his estimated ten minutes and stopped for a drink of water. As he unzipped the bag and reached inside, he could feel the mass of the gun in the outer pocket press against his hand.

"I forgot I had that in there."

You're lucky the damn thing didn't go off when the bag hit the floor.

"That's why you never keep a round in the chamber." James pulled the pistol out of the pocket. He made sure the safety was on and the magazine was properly seated, and then tucked it in his jeans at the small of his back. "I should keep this handy—you know, in case of snakes."

The two-legged kind?

James pushed the bill of his hat up and surveyed the area. The parallel ruts continued along the top of the ridge for another thirty yards before dropping into the next valley. A strip of green made its way along the base of the hill. The trees and grasses stood out against the tan and brown colored desert. His eyes followed the emerald path up to the head of the canyon, where it terminated under a limestone rock formation.

"It looks like there's probably a spring. Maybe I can get water down there."

You have more than enough water to make it out if you turn around right now.

"Still, it's good to know where it is in case of emergency."

You know what else is probably down there?

"Yeah," James looked at the ground in front of his feet, "whoever made these tracks. It could be campers or hunters, but I don't think so. This is a perfect place to grow something."

James hadn't been able to learn much about the Green Legion through his research, but he did learn a few things about how marijuana growers in the area operated. Some would find a spring and plant their seeds in the sheltered canyons fed by the natural water source. Others would bury irrigation tubing to divert the flow to different, less obvious areas. Some went so far as to use batteries charged by solar cells to power timers and valves that irrigated the crops.

I think you've seen enough. It's time to get your butt outta here.

"I agree, but I need to send that message first."

James checked his phone. The signal was still weak, but better than before, so he tried resending the text to Will. Getting no error this time, he pocketed the phone, turned around, and headed back down the hill. As he passed Nigel, he paused for a moment and put a hand on the hood.

"I'll be back for you . . . I promise."

It's a busted car, Jimmy, not a horse that came up lame. It'll be fine.

For the next hour James plodded down the path, scanning from side to side as he went. Fear began to creep into his mind as the reality of his situation settled in. Whenever he heard a noise under one of the bushes, he jumped to the opposite side of the trail. Every bird, rabbit and lizard that moved conjured up images of huge rattlesnakes in his mind. The rustling of the hot breeze through the desert vegetation had the same effect. Several times he found himself reaching behind his back for the gun.

If you don't relax, you're gonna shoot yourself in the ass. Just stick to the middle of the road and you'll be fine.

James followed the advice, picking up his pace as well. As he neared the fork where he made his turn, another sound caught his attention. It wasn't a desert creature this time, but the rumble of a vehicle approaching from behind. He turned around just in time to see a tan, four-wheel drive pickup with two men inside round the corner. James stepped to the side as the truck came to a stop. An older man leaned out the open window and held up a fist with his thumb pointed back up the hill.

"That your Rover back there?"

James nodded and swallowed the dust in his throat. "Yeah, I hit something and broke the battery. I was walking back to the gravel pit to call for some help."

"That's quite a hike." The man stroked his gray beard. "Give ya a lift?"

You realize where these guys just came from, right?

"Thanks." James walked around the back of the truck as the other man opened the passenger door and scooted to the middle. "I appreciate it."

"Not a problem," the driver replied. "Only one road outta here, so we go right past there. I'd go back and tow you out, but we gotta be someplace."

"That's okay. I can get my brother to pull me out with his Jeep."

James glanced at the canvas covered bed as he climbed into the cab. While setting his cooler on the floor between his feet, an odd smell caught his attention—like the truck had hit a skunk. The old man pushed the bill of his cap up, put the truck in gear and started moving again.

"So, what brings you out here?"

"Just doing some exploring." James felt the gun dig into his back as the truck bounced along the trail. He tried his best not to react and give away its presence. "The desert's beautiful this time of year."

In August? Really? Just keep your mouth shut, Jimmy.

"You're lucky we came along." The old man shook his head. "Not good to run around these mountains alone. A lot of people get lost and die out here."

Was that a warning?

"Most of the time they don't even find the bodies," the second man added.

That sounded more like a threat!

James felt his stomach tighten. His mind started racing as he ran through every possible scenario to get out of the truck alive. He almost opened the door and bailed out when the man in the cowboy hat next to him reached toward him, half smiling.

"I'm Ben," he said taking James' trembling hand and shaking it. "This is my Uncle Walt."

Chapter 25

A light spray of water kicked up off the tires as Missy drove through downtown Phoenix. The sudden late morning storm had dropped over half an inch of rain in no more than thirty minutes. It caused many of the main streets to run like rivers. The water subsided just as fast, leaving behind a thin sheet of moisture and a fresh smell in the air.

She pulled the car into the driveway of James' house, grabbed the plastic bag off the seat next to her, and trotted up to the front door. Missy rang the doorbell and waited, but there was no response.

Must be in the bathroom, she thought as she slipped her key in the door and entered the house.

"Jimmy! Where are you? I brought you lunch."

Missy dropped the bag on the dining room table along with her keys, and headed down the hall. Every room was in its usual condition—neat as a pin—but there was no sign of James. Returning to the front of the house, she grabbed the bag off the table and put it in the refrigerator.

"I wonder where he went?" She stood at the sink and looked out the window. "The garage! I'll bet he's tinkering with Nigel again instead of working. Simon's gonna be pissed if he misses a deadline."

Missy went out the back door and walked across the yard to the garage. She gripped the doorknob and tried to turn it—the door was locked. Stepping to the side, she cupped her hands around her face and pressed them against the window. She was surprised to find nothing but empty space where the Land Rover usually sat. She pulled her phone out of her hip pocket and went back in the house. Missy dialed her boyfriend's number, but it went straight to voicemail.

"Jimmy, where are you? Please tell me you're only taking Nigel for a spin around the block. We need to get those new tires before you go too far. I left you some lunch in the fridge. Call me when you get this message, okay? Love ya!"

She slipped the phone back in her pocket and picked her keys up off the table. Before going out the door, she stopped and doubled back toward the desk.

"Maybe I should leave him a note."

Missy pulled out the top drawer and shook her head. James had all of the writing instruments neatly arranged by color, size and function. Even the highlighters were lined up side by side, forming a perfect spectrum with no color out of place. As she picked up a pen and note pad, an irresistible urge came over her. She quickly swapped the red and orange markers, throwing the rainbow out of balance. With a mischievous smile on her face, she slid the drawer back in.

"That ought to drive him crazy!"

She sat down and pushed the keyboard to one side to make some room. As she moved the mouse in the other direction, the computer's monitor lit up. Missy looked up expecting to see an unfinished article, but instead found an open browser window filled by a satellite map. The image was pixilated and blurred, like the magnification had been pushed to its maximum. Curious, she grabbed the mouse and zoomed the image out. Missy felt her stomach push up into her throat when she recognized the location.

"Oh, no! *No, no, no!*" She jumped out of the chair and took a huge step back. "Please tell me you did *not* go out there!"

Missy pulled her phone out and tried James' number again, but it still went to voicemail. She threw her phone at the couch and stomped around the room before throwing her hands in the air.

"The pub! Yeah, he probably went to the pub for lunch!" She retrieved her phone, grabbed her keys, and ran out the door, slamming it behind her.

The drive from James' house to Dugan's usually took fifteen to twenty minutes, depending on the traffic and stoplights—Missy made it in a little less than ten. She circled the parking lot, looking for the faded old Rover but it was nowhere in sight. She whipped the Buick into a space, ran through the door of the pub, and headed straight for the bar.

"Where's the fire?" Donny grinned. "You look like—"

Missy cut him off. "Have you seen Jimmy today? *Please* tell me he's here!"

"Not anymore," he replied. "Haven't seen him since he borrowed the GPS outta my truck this morning."

"Why does he need a GPS? He's got one on his phone."

"I asked him the same thing—said he might be somewhere he can't get a signal."

"Did he tell you where he was going?"

"Nope. Just told me he was gonna do a little exploring. Something wrong?"

"He's not answering his phone." Missy plopped down on a stool, propped her elbows on the bar, and planted her face in her hands. "I think Jimmy might have done something really stupid."

"Jimmy do something stupid?" Donny scoffed. "Willy maybe, but not our Jimmy."

"Will!" Missy sat straight up. "That's it! That *bastard* has him doing some cop thing for him again!"

Donny shrugged his shoulders. "Wouldn't surprise me a bit."

Missy pulled her phone out and dialed Will's number. "I swear, if one hair on Jimmy's head gets hurt . . ."

***

Will and Nestor stepped out of the elevator into the squad room at Phoenix PD.

"I appreciate the ride, but I could've walked back," Will said as they passed by rows of cubicles. "The storm's been over with for more than an hour."

"Why walk? I was coming here to say hello to Detective Stiverson anyway," Nestor replied. "I think you like doing things the hard way."

"Damn right he does." Carl stood up and shook Nestor's hand. "Nice to see you again, Yazzi."

Nestor smiled as he gripped Carl's hand. "How have you been, Jackrabbit?"

"*Jackrabbit?*" Will laughed as he dropped into his chair. "Did he just call you *Jackrabbit?*"

"You bet he did." Carl kicked at Will's foot. "I used to be a lot faster before you started losing bets and paying me off with burritos."

Nestor nodded. "I watched him run down a young buck half his age. Very impressive."

"Do you give everybody nicknames, Yazzi?" Will laughed and shook his head. "Carl's Jackrabbit, McCarthy's Stray Dog . . . how come you haven't pinned a name on me yet?"

"You said he called you pigheaded." Carl grinned at Nestor. "Did you really call him that? 'Cause it's right on the money."

"I did say that when we first met," Nestor replied. "But the more I learn, the more I think Packrat would be more fitting. He turns loose of nothing—carries the burdens of the past with him everywhere he goes."

"What do you know about my past?" Will scoffed. "We've only met a couple of times."

"It's my job to know who I'm working with . . . who I can trust to have my back." Nestor put a hand on Will's shoulder and lowered his head. "I know about your father."

"Then you also know it's over with." Will brushed his hand off. "I caught the son of a bitch a long time ago."

"Yeah, but Yazzi's right. You still ain't over it." Carl looked at Nestor. "That's the fuel that feeds his engine."

Will squirmed in his chair as he turned away. "Can we change the subject, please?"

"Okay," Nestor replied. "Let's talk about Dr. O'Donnell."

Will spun his chair back around with a jerk. "What about her?"

"Her?" Carl pulled another chair over for Nestor. "Have a seat, Yazzi. Any woman that gets a reaction like that outta our little Packrat—well, I gotta know the details."

"She's the Medical Examiner from Prescott," Will snapped. "That's all."

Nestor smiled as he sat down and poked Will in the bicep. "Your boy has a weakness for young women with green eyes and red hair."

"Green eyes, red hair, Irish name . . . and a doctor too?" Carl leaned back and whistled. "Your mama's gonna *love* her!"

"I don't think the doctor was very impressed, Carl." Nestor mugged a frown as he teased Will. "Packrat's mouth got ahead of his brain."

Will's face blushed beet-red. "Cut it out, guys. You sound like a couple of high school girls gossiping behind the bleachers."

"So, you gonna ask her to the prom?" Carl busted out in a full-on belly laugh. It didn't take long for Nestor to crack and join in as well.

"Coupla goddamn comedians." Will felt his cell phone vibrate in his pocket. "I'm gonna go ahead and take this call while you guys get your shit together."

Will stood up and walked to the window at the end of the row before answering.

"Detective Dugan"

"WHAT THE HELL HAVE YOU DONE WITH JIMMY?"

Missy's voice was so loud it sounded like the phone was on speaker. Will ripped it away from his ear and held it at arms length until she finished yelling. He cautiously moved the phone closer before answering.

"What are you talking about? Jimmy's fine." He put the phone back up to his ear. "You were at the house when I dropped him off last night."

Missy lowered her volume. "You don't have him running around doing more of your dirty work?"

"I have no idea what you're talking about."

"Jimmy's gone," Missy took a breath, "and so is Nigel."

Will shook his head. "Did you try to call him? He probably just went to Mom's for lunch."

"I'm *at* the bar, Detective Dumbass! He's not here, but Donny said he came by this morning to borrow his GPS."

Will raised one eyebrow. "What does he need a GPS for?"

Missy hesitated before answering. "He left a satellite map open on his computer. I think he went out to look at Ben's property."

"WHAT?" Will's voice carried throughout the room. "Stay where you are. I'm on my way!"

Will looked at his phone as he hung up the call and saw a text alert at the top of the screen. He tapped on the icon to open it. The message was over an hour old.

JAMES: Car broke down. West Table Mesa Road. Hiking out.

"*Dammit!*" Will turned back toward the two senior officers. "Guys, I think we might have a problem . . ."

Chapter 26

As soon as Will rounded the corner into the parking lot of Dugan's, Missy ran out the front door. She didn't even wait for the open topped Jeep to come to a complete stop before jumping into the passenger side and grabbing the seatbelt.

"What the hell are you doing?" Will whipped into a space. "You're not coming with me. I just came by to see what you found at Jimmy's and give you an update before I go track him down."

"You can update me on the way out there." Missy fastened the belt and gritted her teeth. "Put this damn thing in gear and get a move on! We gotta find him before he gets himself in trouble!"

"Too late, he's *already* in trouble." Will turned around and pulled back out on the street. "He sent me a text while I was in a meeting. My phone was turned down, so I didn't see it until you called."

"What happened?" Missy grabbed Will's arm tight enough to leave marks. "Where is he? Is he okay?"

"That piece of British crap you guys have been playing with broke down. He's somewhere off Table Mesa Road, hiking out."

"Dammit!" Missy let go of Will's arm and grabbed the handle on the dash as they skidded around a corner. "I told Jimmy Nigel wasn't ready to go off-road yet!"

"That's the *least* of my worries, sister." He swung a hard right and shifted into high gear as they weaved through traffic. "I'm more concerned with the road he decided to take his little adventure on. If the wrong person catches him out there, we might be looking in a mineshaft for *his* body."

Missy slapped his arm. "I didn't need to hear that!" She twisted back into her seat. "Even if he doesn't run into anybody, he could still die from dehydration or something."

Will shook his head. "I doubt it. Knowing Jimmy, he'll be prepared. He's smart enough not to head out there without food and water."

"Really?" Missy glared at Will. "He went out into the desert alone—in a forty-year-old rust-bucket—so he could poke around the property owned by a guy who *might* have killed a dozen people. It sounds to me like Jimmy's not in *smart-mode* right now. Come to think of it, he's acting like *you*!"

Will threw up a hand. "Hey, this one's not on me!"

"You're the one that's got him playing cop all the time." She pointed an accusing finger. "If you did your job instead of conning Jimmy into doing it for you . . ."

"I didn't con anybody, and I didn't tell him to go off chasing leads on his own." Will turned onto the freeway ramp and floored the accelerator between shifts, jerking both of them back in their seats. "I don't know what the hell's gotten into him."

"*You've* gotten into him!" Missy balled up her fist and shook it at Will. "*You* took him out in the desert chasing bodies, *you* made him pose as a drug dealer—*you* even gave him a gun!"

"I didn't *give* him a gun," Will protested. "I just asked him to stash it for me. Besides, *you're* the one that taught him how to use one."

Missy cocked her arm back. "If you weren't driving right now I'd—"

"Why is beating the hell out of me always your go-to response?" Will glowered at her. "That's not gonna fix anything, and you know it. We need to concentrate on finding Jimmy before he gets in any deeper."

Missy lowered her fist. "And just how are we gonna do that?"

"If you're right about the map he had up on his computer we know what he was aiming for. If we're lucky, maybe he broke down *before* he got to Weber's property."

"And if he didn't? What if he decided to go back up to that mine and got lost?"

"He's not lost." Will pointed at the screen suction-cupped to the windshield. "He has Donny's GPS, remember? And I'm sure he knows to follow his own tracks back out."

"He could still be anywhere. We can't search the whole desert alone." Missy pointed at the dark clouds collecting over the hills to the north. "And what if it starts raining? We need backup."

"Carl's trying to round up some help, and Deputy Yazzi's already headed that direction."

"Oh, great." Missy shook her head. "Isn't he the one that called him a stray dog?"

"Yeah, he was with me when you called. I wouldn't worry about Yazzi, he likes Jimmy." Will reached over and put a hand on her arm. "Listen, I may not get along with that guy, but he knows those mountains—it's his home turf."

"Well, I hope *somebody* gets to Jimmy before something happens." Missy pulled her arm away as a car accelerated past and cut into the lane in front of them. "Can't this thing go any faster? And don't you have a siren and one of those little swirly lights?"

"It's a Jeep, not a muscle car. I've got it all the way to the floor." Will pushed down harder on the pedal. "And I don't have a siren. I usually work undercover, remember?"

"I'm worried about him, Will. He's never done anything like this before."

"We need to stop assuming the worst. There's a gravel pit on that road. He'll probably make it that far and find help before we even get out there."

"I hope so."

Missy closed her eyes as the wind whipped her hair in the open Jeep. She did her best to think positive thoughts for the rest of the ride. She tried to picture James happily strolling down a dirt road, whistling a march in time with his steps as they approached. It didn't work. As they passed New River, she pulled out her phone and checked it for the tenth time.

"So, how come we haven't heard from him yet?"

"Maybe the battery on his phone died."

"If he made it to the gravel pit, he could have borrowed one."

Will thought for a second. "Maybe they can't get a signal there. It is down in a low area."

"You're just *full* of answers," Missy huffed. "It's a business. Won't they have a land line?"

"I doubt there's any phone lines running out there, but we're about to find out." Will pulled off the exit ramp and turned west. "The pit's only a couple miles down the road."

Missy looked at the surrounding desert and up at the building clouds. "What if he's not there?"

"Then we keep going until we find him. Next logical place to look would be Weber's property."

"Logical?" Missy half smiled. "Now you're sounding like Jimmy."

Will grinned. "Guess we're picking up each other's bad habits."

He slowed down where the paved road turned to dirt. They continued down into the valley and through a couple of washes, kicking up a plume of dust as the Jeep bounced over the washboard surface. They rounded a corner and the gravel pit came into view. Missy frowned and turned toward Will as he brought the car to a stop. The gate to the area was closed, secured by a heavy length of chain and a large padlock.

"This isn't good," Missy sighed. "It means Jimmy's still out there somewhere."

Will nodded. "Let's head for Weber's."

"Do you know how to get there?" Missy asked. "It's not going to help Jimmy if we get lost too."

"Before I left the precinct, I grabbed the map Jimmy sent me." Will pointed at the glove compartment as he pulled the Jeep back onto the dirt road. "You're on navigator duty."

Missy pulled the paper out and studied it. "Looks pretty easy to find." She pointed at the GPS. "Go left at that next fork. It's maybe another mile and a half after that to Ben's place."

"Is that all?" Will followed her instructions. "That means he must have gone past it. It's been almost two hours since he sent that text. If he was just another mile or two down the road, he could have walked all the way to the highway by now."

"Maybe he did." Missy looked at the map again. "He could have thumbed a ride back into town."

Will shook his head. "I don't see Jimmy hitchhiking on the side of the freeway—and we would've heard from him by now. No, he's still out there somewhere."

Missy checked her phone again. "You were right about not getting a signal. We're almost to the property, so he couldn't have texted you from here."

"He would've had to do it from higher ground." Will pointed at a ridge to the west. "Maybe up there somewhere."

Missy motioned toward the left side of the road. "This is Ben's property . . . and I don't see Nigel."

Will stopped the Jeep and hopped out. He reached into a pack behind the seat, pulled out a pair of binoculars, and scanned the ridge. Missy put the map back, jumped out the other side, and walked around the front of the vehicle. Something on the ground caught her eye.

"Will! Look at this!" She pointed at a set of tire tracks off to the side of the road. "Jimmy's been here!"

Will tossed the binoculars on the seat and ran to where Missy was standing. He dropped down on one knee to inspect the impressions in the loose dirt.

"How do you know these tracks are Jimmy's?"

"Look at the patterns—the tires are mismatched. And see that funky looking spot?" Missy pointed at a crescent shaped mark in one of the impressions. "Nigel has one odd tire with a chunk out of the tread."

"I see footprints headed across the road." Will stood up and followed the prints. "Looks like he headed straight for that pile of brush."

Missy fell in behind him as they followed the tracks. When they reached the pile, Will pulled a few of the branches back, exposing one of the doors to the buried shipping container.

"That fat little *weasel*!" Missy planted her hands on her hips and stomped her foot. "He *is* in the business!"

"We don't know that yet. He could just be one of those nutcase doomsday preppers."

Missy pointed at the padlock. "Shoot that damn thing off! I want to see what Ben's got in there!"

Will shook his head as he put the branches back in place. "They only do that on TV. I have bolt cutters in the Jeep, but since we don't have a warrant and we're way out of my jurisdiction, I think we'll leave this one to Yazzi."

"How are you gonna reach him? We can't get a signal."

"I've got a radio in my pack," Will replied as they trotted back to the car. "Worst case, I still have the satellite phone."

Missy climbed back into the Jeep and buckled her belt. "So, what now?"

"We know Jimmy's been poking around out here. Somebody else might've figured that out too." Will started the engine, leaned back in the seat and rubbed his face with both palms. He sighed as he turned his head. "I'd say our top priority is to find him before Weber does."

Missy pulled the map back out of the glove box as Will put the Jeep in gear and started driving again.

"It looks like the road doesn't split until we get to the other side of the river. We can look for his tracks there to see which way he went."

"Yeah, if the rain holds off and wind doesn't blow 'em away." Will nodded toward a cloud of dust rising in the distance as the road turned and dropped in to the dry riverbed. "Looks like somebody's coming."

"Is it Jimmy?" Missy craned her neck and strained to see. "Maybe he got Nigel running!"

"Wrong color," Will replied. "And it's a pickup."

"That kinda looks like Uncle Walt's old truck." Missy's eyes grew wide as the truck got closer. She gasped and grabbed Will's arm. *"Oh my God! Did you see that?"*

"Son-of-a-bitch!" He hit the accelerator, reached behind the seat, and fished the radio out of his pack.

"I'll call it in!"

Chapter 27

James stared straight ahead as the truck bounced along the dirt road. He sat next to a portly cowboy named Ben. Walt, the man's uncle, was behind the wheel. James tried his best not to make eye contact with either of them. There was no doubt in his mind who these men were, but of all the people he could have encountered in the desert foothills of the Bradshaw Mountains, he wondered, why did it have to be them? What were the odds? Of course, Josh had an answer.

Considering where you decided to go poking around, the odds were pretty good.

Ben turned his head and squinted as he eyed James up and down. "What'd you say your name was?"

"Ja . . . Jim, my name is Jim." There was a slight quiver in his voice.

"You look familiar." He studied James' profile. "Ever hang out at the Yacht Club in Cleator?"

James turned away and looked out the open window. "I've never heard of Cleator. Is that somewhere around Lake Pleasant?"

"Farther north." Ben pointed over his shoulder. "On the road between Bumblebee and Crown King."

James had a puzzled look. "I don't remember seeing another lake up that direction on the map."

"There ain't one. Kind of an inside joke." Ben continued to stare at him. "I swear I've seen your face somewhere before."

"I doubt we've met." James tried his best to sound indifferent. "I don't get out of the city much."

"Then I guess it musta been somewhere in town." Ben thought for a moment, and then snapped his fingers. "The Outdoor Expo at the convention center.

You were signin' books there a couple weeks ago. You're Josh McDaniel!"

Uh-oh, Jimmy! Think fast!

"I *was* at the expo, but I'm not Josh McDaniel." James tried to force a smile. "I've been told I kind of look like him, but he's taller and more muscular."

"Couldn't tell with him sittin' down behind that table." Ben shook his head. "But I swear, you put the razor down for a couple days, you'd look just like the guy."

Walt looked over and gave a slight nod. "Ben's right—you got the same eyes."

"Maybe we're distant cousins or something." James shrugged his shoulders. "Anyway, I've read a few of his books. He probably would have had some trick to fix the Rover. A guy like that wouldn't have to walk back to civilization."

"Yeah, he comes off as pretty resourceful." Walt muscled the steering wheel as the truck crawled down the hill into the riverbed. "Probably wouldn't have headed out in the middle of nowhere without a toolbox and some kinda survival gear either."

Or I would have followed the number one rule of survival and stayed with the vehicle.

Ben pushed the brim of his hat up. "What busted on the Rover, Jim?"

"The battery." James frowned. "I hit a rock and the mount broke. It ripped the positive post out when it fell."

Walt scratched the back of head and then straightened his cap. "That thing looked pretty old. Does it have a generator or an alternator under the hood?"

"It's a generator. We just put a rebuilt one in last week." James looked confused. "Does that make a difference?"

Walt dipped his chin. "Damn right it does. Don't need a battery to keep it runnin' with a generator. Just make sure nothin's shorted out, turn the key on, and get it rollin' down hill. When you get some speed, slam it in gear and pop the clutch."

James lowered his head. "I didn't even think of that."

"Guess that proves it," Ben laughed. "You ain't Josh McDaniel."

No you're not, but to be perfectly honest, I didn't think of that either.

"I guess I'm lucky you came along. I really didn't think I'd see anyone. That's why I started walking." As James turned to look at Walt, the tarp covered bed caught his eye. "So, what brings you guys out here?"

Don't go there, Jimmy . . .

Ben's smile faded. "Why do you wanna know?"

"Just curious." James shrugged his shoulders and tried to look innocent. "Like I said, I didn't expect to see anyone out here, especially in the middle of the week."

Are you trying to tick this guy off?

Ben started to slide his left hand under the front edge of the seat, but Walt caught him by the wrist and raised one eyebrow. The look was subtle, but James picked up on it and retreated against the door. Ben put his hand back in his lap.

"Just out doin' a little prospectin'." Walt gave Ben a stern look. "Sorry about my nephew. He gets a little nervous sometimes—thinks everybody's a claim-jumper."

"You don't have to worry about me." James relaxed his posture a little, but kept a hand on the armrest close to the door's latch. "I wouldn't even know where to start looking for gold."

Yeah, right. You've written three articles on it, but I wouldn't tell them that.

A frown was still locked on Ben's face. "So you're just out here drivin' around, huh? Why'd you pick *this* area?"

"I've never been down this road before. I wanted to see where it goes."

"It don't go *anywhere*," Ben snapped. "Just dead ends halfway up the mountain. Nothin' to see up there."

"I figured it might lead to an old mine or something," James waved his hand out the window. "I've heard these hills are full of them."

Ben didn't look convinced. "Why are you trying to find old mines? You said you're not interested in gold. You lookin' for somethin' else?"

Back it down a little, Jimmy. You're making him nervous.

"I wasn't looking for anything specific." James put his hand back down near the latch again. "I just got the Rover running and I wanted to see how it would do off the pavement."

"Guess you shoulda stuck a little closer to home." The truck kicked up a tail of dust as Walt guided it through the sandy river bottom. "Tell anybody where you were goin'?"

James shook his head. "No, it was kind of a last-minute thing."

Ben glared at him. "So, nobody knows where to look for you?"

I don't like where this is going . . .

"Not a clue." James decided it was best not to mention the one text he had been able to send. "They don't even know I'm gone."

He watched out of the corner of his eye as Ben and Walt exchanged looks. It was as if they were having a debate, but without words. The longer the unspoken conversation went on, the more nervous he got. Did they suspect why he was really out here? Had they figured out he really *was* the man they'd seen at the expo? James couldn't take the silence any longer.

"Maybe I should try to let my family know where I am." He reached down and started to slide the phone out of his pocket, but Walt held up a hand.

"Won't do any good down here in the bottom." He pointed at the high banks and hills surrounding the riverbed. "We're between the ridges. You can't get a signal 'til we get up the hill on the other side of the quarry."

"I guess I'll have to wait. "James pushed the phone back into his pocket. "Do you spend a lot of time out here? You seem to know the area pretty well, even where the phones work"

"And you ask a lotta questions for a guy runnin' around the desert lookin' for nothin'." The corners of Walt's mouth pulled down. "What are you *really* doin' out here?"

Nice job, now they're both pissed!

"Honest, Mr. Franklin, I was just driving around." James felt his stomach crawling up his throat as Ben slipped his hand off his lap again. "I'm not trying to jump anyone's claim."

Walt slowed the truck down and scowled as he turned to look James in the eye. "What did you just call me?"

James swallowed hard. "M-Mr. Franklin . . ."

"How did you know my name?"

"Um . . . you . . . um . . . Ben said it when you first picked me up."

Ben shook his head. "I just called him Uncle Walt. I never said his *last* name."

Oh Shit . . .

Chapter 28

James sat frozen against the door. Both men stared at him with fire in their eyes. He was stuck in a moving pickup with two suspected murderers and no easy way out. His mouth hung wide open. Try as he might, he could not form words, or even a cogent thought. Josh remained silent as well. This time when Ben reached under the edge of the seat, Walt made no move to stop him. When he pulled his hand back up, James caught a flash of light off of chrome.

As Ben raised the barrel of the revolver, James felt something akin to an electric shock travel through every cell in his body. His vision blurred. Instinct and adrenaline took over. Without thinking, he pulled the latch on the door and dove from the moving truck, tumbling as he hit the sandy river-bottom. He sprang to his feet and tried to run, but found himself face down on the ground again. He looked at his legs—he was tangled up in the shoulder strap of the cooler that had been sitting between his feet.

Walt slammed on the brakes and the truck skidded, kicking up a cloud of dust. The sudden stop sent Ben sideways into the dash, knocking his gun out of his hand. He quickly regained his composure, scooped up the weapon, and jumped out of the open door. Walt grabbed his pistol from the pocket in the driver's door before bailing out of the other side.

James kicked at the cooler and managed to free himself from the strap. He flopped onto his back when Ben came around the corner of the truck. As James squirmed on the ground, he felt something dig into him just below his kidney.

The gun! You've still got the gun, dammit! Use it!

James reached around and pulled the small .25 automatic out as he rolled onto his stomach. He racked the slide, aimed at Ben, and squeezed the trigger—the bullet missed its mark and struck the tailgate. Ben and Walt both hit the ground and rolled behind opposite sides of the truck. James scrambled to get to his feet and ran into the brush and up the embankment along the edge of the riverbed, his ears still ringing from the report of the gun. Keeping a low profile, he dodged between the rocks and cactus, glancing back toward the truck whenever he passed an opening in the bushes. James caught a glimpse of Ben and Walt, both back on their feet and headed in his direction.

As he looked to the north, a narrow shaft of sunlight split the clouds and shined like a spotlight on something coming down the road. A red vehicle was powering through the sand, throwing a rooster-tail high in the air behind it. James squatted down behind a large boulder and tried to catch his breath, the gun still clutched in his right hand. He wanted desperately to see if it was his brother's Jeep, but didn't dare give away his position. As the voices of his pursuers grew closer, James pressed his body against the rock. He could hear Ben fighting to breathe.

"Did you . . . see . . . which way . . . he went?"

"Probably headed for higher ground," Walt growled back. "You keep after him. I'll go get the truck and see if I can cut him off on the other side of the hill."

James heard footsteps going off in opposite directions. He waited until the sound of Ben's huffing faded before creeping around the boulder and sneaking a look between a couple of mesquite trees. His heart jumped when he saw Will bail out of the Jeep, gun drawn and pointed in the direction of a surprised Walter Franklin. Walt tossed his weapon to the side, raised his arms above his head, and dropped to his knees.

Will pulled a set of handcuffs out of his back pocket as he approached, but before he had a chance to use them, Walt got another surprise. Missy appeared from behind the Jeep and ran straight at him. She landed a flying kick directly in the center of her uncle's chest, knocking him on his back. Before Will could react, she was on top of the man, her knees pinning his arms down as she landed several punches to his face. She was screaming so loud James could hear every word cut through the air from a hundred yards away.

"You God-damned-son-of-a-bitch!" She punctuated her sentence with another blow. "You let my brother go to jail!" She hit him again. "You lied about quitting the Legion!" Another fist found his nose. "Now you're trying to kill my boyfriend?"

Will holstered his gun and grabbed her around the waist, pulling her off the bloodied old man. Missy kicked and flailed as he dropped her on her feet.

"He's done, Missy! Let him go!"

He sat Walt up and leaned him against the truck before cuffing him to a bracket under the fender well. Will inspected the damage to the man's face.

"Jesus! You almost *killed* him!"

Walt's gun lay half buried in the sand where he dropped it. Missy took a couple steps toward the weapon and reached down. Will caught her again and spun her around.

"What the hell do think you're doing? That's evidence. Don't touch it!"

"Ben's still out there going after Jimmy!" Missy balled up her fists again. "I'm gonna track that little bastard and *shoot* his ass!"

"Like *hell* you are. You leave Weber to me." Will pointed at the ground in front of her. "You're gonna stay *right* here!"

Walt looked up through his swollen eyes and growled. "You leave that bitch here and I'll be dead before you get back."

"You wish!" Missy kicked her uncle in the calf, then crossed her arms and stood over him. "I'm gonna *love* watching you rot in jail!"

"You keep an eye on him." Will smiled, slipped a lock blade knife out of his pocket and handed it to her. "If he gets outta line, do what you gotta do. Just leave something for the vultures, okay?"

Will pulled his weapon, ran to where Ben's tracks entered the brush, and disappeared into the desert. James had a strong urge to stand up and call out to his brother. He also wanted to run to Missy, desperate to let her know he was okay.

You want to let Weber know, too? Keep your damn head down!

James obeyed his inner voice this time and kept low. He tried to work his way back toward Will, careful not to make too much noise. As he raised his head just enough to get his bearings, he heard something whiz past him. Milliseconds later, a loud BOOM slapped his ears.

James hit the ground and pointed his gun in the direction of the sound. Ben was about thirty yards away, bounding down the hill after him. He fired again, striking a cactus to James' left. James took aim and returned fire. The bullet grazed the wide brim of Ben's hat. James pulled the trigger again, but nothing happened. He looked at the pistol. A cartridge was stove-piped in the slide. He reached up to clear the misfire, but it was too late. Ben was only a few yards away now. James could see the gaping mouth of the revolver's barrel pointed directly at his face.

Time slowed down as James closed his eyes and gritted his teeth. He waited for the sound of the gun and the searing pain he knew would follow. It never came. Instead, he heard a loud *thwack*, followed by a distant *crack* that echoed off the surrounding hills. When James opened his eyes again, he was surprised to see Ben in a fetal position on the ground clutching his left forearm and screaming, blood oozing between his fingers. More of the crimson liquid was spattered on the brush and cactus next to him. The chrome revolver lay between the spiny leaves of a yucca plant.

James got to his feet and scanned the horizon in the direction the shot appeared to have come from. Standing on the top of a hill some 300 yards away, he saw the stocky figure of Nestor Yazzi holding a scoped rifle in one hand and waving his hat with the other. A moment later he felt a pair of arms wrap around him from the side and squeeze hard, almost lifting him off the ground. He turned his head expecting to see Missy, but found Will instead.

"I thought you were *dead*, brother!" He released James and waved back at Yazzi. "God bless that damned Indian! That was one *hell* of a shot!"

James stood in shock, the gun still tight in his hand. Will reached down, gently peeled his brother's fingers off the grip, and took the weapon.

"I missed," James said slowly. "Gun jammed."

"Guess you were right about the whole revolver thing." Will laughed, trying to lighten the moment as he inspected the pistol. "These things have a tendency to suck when you roll 'em around in a sandbox."

James pointed at the whimpering figure writhing on the ground in front of them. His expression was flat, his voice emotionless.

"He almost killed me." James dropped to his knees, his unblinking stare locked on Weber and the pool of blood growing under him.

"You gonna be alright?" Will put a hand on his brother's shoulder. "Just breathe, Jimmy. It'll take a little time, but you'll get through this."

James took a deep breath. "Is he dying?"

"Nah, he'll live." Will unbuckled his belt and pulled it out of its loops. "Cavalry's on the way. Help me get a tourniquet on him so he doesn't bleed out before they get here."

James stood up and took a step back. His eyes widened as he looked at Will, but nothing came out of his mouth. Will gave a single nod and knelt down next to Weber.

"I'll take care of this. You go check on your girlfriend."

Chapter 29

James sat quietly on the tailgate of Nestor's truck. Missy was glued to his side, arms wrapped tight around his torso. Her eyes were red and puffy, her knuckles bruised and swollen. They watched a medical helicopter lift off the ground in the distance. It blasted up a cloud of sand and dirt, engulfing the surrounding officers and vehicles now lining the riverbed. The aircraft banked and headed south under the heavy gray clouds.

"I'm sorry, Jimmy." Missy rested her head on his shoulder. "I'm sure you hate me right now."

James stroked her hair. "Why would I hate you?"

"Because of my family." She sniffed and cleared her throat. "I should've told you about all of this shit a long time ago, but I didn't want to lose you."

"You're not going to lose me. It's not like *you* were doing anything wrong. It was your uncle—and you didn't even know your cousin was involved. We never would have made that connection if you hadn't spoken up."

"And you never would have ended up out here getting shot at either."

"That's my fault." James held her tighter. "I shouldn't have come out here alone. I guess I really shouldn't have come out here at all."

"We finally agree on something." Will stood in front of them, arms folded across his chest. "What made you think you needed to go poking a stick in this hornet's nest by yourself?"

"I wanted to find out what Missy's cousin had on his property. I was trying to clear her family." James hung his head. "I hoped I wouldn't find anything."

"Well, it was a stupid move," Will barked. "You're not a cop, Jimmy."

Missy jumped up and stood toe to toe with Will. "Then why do you keep using him like he *is* one?"

"That's different." Will held his ground. "I've never put him in a situation where I wasn't there to back him up."

"It's true, Missy." James pulled her back toward him and gently cradled her injured hands. "And when we went to see Ronny Perez, he told me to stay hidden and not get involved at all. It was my choice to step in, not his."

"If you hadn't picked up that gun, the guy would've killed him." Missy turned her head and glared at Will. "You owe him *big-time*."

"Yeah, about that gun." Will kicked at the dirt. "Since you discharged it out here today, that thing is evidence now. They're probably gonna ask where you got it. Go ahead and be honest. Tell 'em I gave it to you."

James cocked his head. "Won't you get in trouble when they find out where it *really* came from?"

"They won't ask about that." Will half smiled. "They don't want to know the answer. Every cop has a couple extra guns stashed, especially the guys who work undercover. Nobody wants to know where they got 'em."

"What about Ben's property?" James looked up to where the road climbed back out of the riverbed. "What did they find in the shipping container he has buried up there?"

"Nothing yet. They'll have to wait for a warrant before they open it." Will pointed at the back of Walt's truck. "Based on what's under that tarp, I don't think there's gonna be a problem getting one."

Missy frowned. "Is that what I think it is?"

"If you're thinking they just harvested a bumper crop of high grade bud, then yeah, it's exactly what you think it is."

"I can't believe this." She sighed and sat back down. "Are you sure they killed all those people? I know they were growing and selling, but couldn't another member of the Legion be responsible for the murders?"

"Can't say for sure until we check out the weapons." Will shifted his weight from one foot to the other a few times. "But it doesn't look good."

"Not good at all." Deputy Yazzi walked around the back of the truck and joined the group. "Good call on the guns, Packrat. Alexander's team recovered a .45 caliber revolver and a 9 millimeter Glock."

Missy and James looked at each other and spoke in unison. "*Packrat?*"

"I'll explain later." Will held his hand out toward Nestor. "Wanna bet the ballistics match up with the slugs and casings from the mine?"

Nestor held up both hands, his palms facing Will. "Only a fool would take that bet." He turned to James. "You okay, Stray Dog?"

"Still a little shaky, but I'll be alright." Nestor looked surprised when James stood up and hugged him. "I can't believe you were able to hit Weber's arm from that far away while he was moving. You saved my life."

Nestor patted him on the back and whispered in his ear before releasing him from the embrace. "I've wanted to shoot that man for a long time. Thanks for giving me a good reason."

"That *was* quite a shot." Will shook Nestor's hand and smiled. "I'm guessing Yavapai County doesn't keep an M40-A3 in their arsenal. Do the Marines know that one's missing?"

Nestor grinned. "My hunting rifle."

"Yeah, right," Will laughed. "How many deer have you had to shoot at 800 yards?"

"Never said what I hunt with it." Yazzi winked and then eyed Missy. "I recognize you. You're Melissa Franklin."

"How do you know that? I've never been arrested." She glanced at Will. "Well, almost never . . ."

"I caught you and Stacy Marks drinking in the park up in Mayor. I didn't arrest you; I tried to drive you home."

"That was you?" Missy studied his aging face. "That was almost ten years ago. How did you remember that?"

Nestor smiled. "You made a strong impression. You were a fighter—didn't want to go back to your parents' place."

"I almost gave you a black eye." She lowered her head. "My dad would have done a whole lot worse to me. I wanted you to take me to jail instead."

"You were just doing what teenagers do. Besides, you were over eighteen. I couldn't make you go back there if you didn't want to." Yazzi sat down next to her and took off his hat. "I saw the fear in your eyes. That's why I took you someplace safe. No one should go to jail for being scared."

"You took us to Stacy's house. You even dropped us off down the block so her parents wouldn't see." Missy looked into Nestor's dark eyes. "I never went home after that. I got my brother to pack up some of my stuff and sneak it out of the house."

"I never saw you again. Figured you ran away."

Missy nodded. "I bought a bus ticket a couple days later. That's when I came down to Phoenix. I felt bad for leaving Jake behind, but I couldn't take it anymore."

"I understand." Nestor stared off into the distance. "I've had to deal with your father a few times over the years. I don't blame you for leaving. He gets mean when he drinks."

"He's mean all the time," Missy replied. "It just gets worse with every beer. Mom's not any better."

"I'm glad you broke the cycle." Nestor smiled and motioned toward James. "Stray Dog is a good man."

"Not as good as he thinks he is." Will looked at James and shook his head. "I still don't get why you thought it was a good idea to head off into the hills alone."

James bit his lower lip. "After spending the night out here, then helping you guys find the mine, and . . . well . . . other things, I guess I felt like I could handle it. I never thought I'd run into anyone."

"Or break down and end up in a truck with those two," Will added. "You got in *way* over your head. Face it, Jimmy, you're not ready to solo yet."

"He's right, Stray Dog. For now, you need a guide on your path." Nestor stood and put his hat back on. "You have great knowledge, but experience teaches you things you can't get from books or computers."

"One thing this experience *has* taught me is to not take people at their word." James seemed to wilt as he looked up at Nestor. "Why do people find it so easy to lie? I understand when Will has to do it because he's undercover—that's his job. But Missy's uncle lied to her about getting out of the drug business. He even let her brother go to jail for him instead of telling the truth. How do you do that to your own family?"

Nestor paused and looked around for a moment, then put a hand on James' shoulder and smiled. "That's a hard question, but maybe I have an answer for you. Let's go for a walk."

James stood up, kissed his girlfriend's cheek, and nodded at Nestor. The two men walked down the road at an easy pace, putting some distance between them and the chaotic crime scene. Neither one uttered a word until Yazzi came to a stop and looked at the ground beside James.

"You see that stone?" He pointed at a round rock a little larger than a softball. "Pick it up."

James did as he was told, gripping it with both hands.

"Tell me how it feels, not how much it weighs," Nestor instructed, "just how it feels."

"Kind of rough," James replied. "And heavy."

"Okay, put it down and pick this one up." Nestor pointed out a much bigger piece of broken granite.

James squatted down and hefted the larger rock, struggling under its weight.

"Tell me about this one, Stray Dog."

"Well, it's a lot heavier and it has sharp edges. Holding on to it is hurting my hands."

"Go ahead and put it down." Nestor returned to the smaller stone. "Pick up the first one again."

James dropped the rock and dusted himself off before going back to the other stone. This time he reached down with one hand, grabbed it, and held it out. Nestor took it from him, looking over its surface as he turned it in the air.

"You didn't use two hands this time." He set it on top of the larger rock. "Why?"

James shrugged. "I don't know. I guess it didn't look as heavy after I picked up the other one."

"There's your answer." Nestor smiled and pointed at the stacked rocks. "The smaller stone is the lie Melissa's uncle told; the larger rock is the taking of a life."

James sighed and nodded. "I thought it was going to be more complicated, but I think I get it. He was a drug dealer and a murderer. Compared to that, lying is nothing to him, even if it hurts family."

"Very good, Stray Dog." Nestor bent down and picked up a flat, round pebble about the size of a quarter and placed it in James' palm. "This is the truth. It's the easiest to carry."

James rubbed the pebble between his fingers, feeling its smooth edges. He held it up as a ray of sunlight broke through the clouds and reflected off its surface, polished by centuries of running water. He slipped it into his front pocket without saying a word and smiled.

"You're going to be okay, Stray Dog." Nestor pointed James back up the road to where Missy and Will waited. "How about we go find your car."

Chapter 30

The rumble of a jet taking off from Sky Harbor Airport echoed off the low hanging clouds. It drowned out the sound of the morning traffic passing by on Twelfth Street. Will opened the door to Carolina's and took a deep breath in through his nose. He stopped for a moment and savored the aroma. The smell of stewed meats, Mexican spices, and fresh tortillas never failed to bring a smile to his face. As he stood in the line snaking its way back from the service counter, he felt a heavy hand on his right shoulder. Will turned to see his partner's toothy grin.

"What are you doing here, Doogie?"

Will pointed up at the menu board. "I was gonna buy you breakfast for picking up the slack when I had to take off yesterday."

"I already grabbed us breakfast." Carl held up the bag in his other hand. "Might as well eat it while it's hot. Get us a couple drinks and I'll find a table."

Carl headed into the crowded dining area and managed to secure the last open table. After paying for the drinks, Will swung by the soda fountain to fill them up. He dropped the cups off at the table, then doubled back, grabbed a handful of napkins, and filled a couple of small plastic cups with salsa.

"Why'd you buy me breakfast?" Will asked as he unwrapped his burrito. "You haven't lost a bet in over two years."

"And you haven't lost one in over two days." Carl smiled and picked up one of the salsa cups. "I figured you might need it after yesterday. How's McCarthy doing?"

"Still a little rattled." Will took a bite and talked with his mouth full. "Yazzi did a pretty good job of talking him through things. They took a walk and Jimmy came back with a little more color in his face. I think he'll be okay."

"Had to be tough on the kid," Carl sighed. "As cops we face stuff like that every day, but it's gotta be new territory for him."

Will set his burrito down and wiped egg off his chin with the back of his hand. "I still don't get why he took off on his own like that."

"Well," Carl thought for a moment, "McCarthy was there when you guys found the body, and he was involved in the search when you found that mine. You've had him neck-deep in this thing from the beginning. I'd guess he was just trying to follow it through to the end."

"But without backup?" Will rolled his eyes. "That's not too smart if you ask me."

"Sounds like somebody else I know." Carl smiled and poured salsa on the end of his burrito before taking a bite.

"That's different and you know it. Like you said, I'm a cop—he's not."

"Speaking of cops . . ." Carl wiped his hands and set the napkin back in his lap. "We rounded up Ronny Perez after things calmed down yesterday. I took Jesse with me. He's a good kid—smart too."

Will raised an eyebrow. "You seem to be taking a lot of interest in him lately. Is there something you want to tell me?"

"Like what?"

"Sounds like maybe you're training a new partner."

"Are you kidding?" Carl chuckled. "You put me through hell, Doogie. I'm too close to retirement to go through that shit again. I just figured he might want to be there since it was his first undercover gig that led to the arrest."

Will nodded. "Yeah, I guess he deserved to be there. I wish I could have seen Ronny's face when you guys opened that van."

"Oh he denied any knowledge of the stuff we found in there, even after Jesse said he saw him get into it. Perez swore he was setup."

"Sounds about right. Who did he try to pin it on? The shop owner?" Will smiled and took another bite.

"Some thug named Willy-D . . . and his boss."

Will choked and coughed, sending a spray of food across the table. Carl covered his breakfast with his hands just in time to save it from a shower of eggs and cheese.

"My *boss*?" Will picked up a wad of napkins and started to clean up the mess. "What the hell was he talking about?"

"Perez said the guy with you the other night was your boss. He said after you jumped him, the guy pulled a gun and broke the two of you up."

"He jumped *me*," Will protested. "I had that guy hiding around the corner just in case Ronny did something stupid. Turns out it was a good move."

"Yeah, about that guy." Carl wiped his hands and locked eyes with Will. "Who is he?"

Will shrugged. "Just somebody that owed me a favor."

"I need a name, Doogie," Carl demanded. "Ronny Perez gave me one, but I want to hear it from you."

Will shifted his eyes away. "He's a nobody, Carl."

"That's not what Perez said." Carl leaned in and narrowed his eyes. "He said the guy's name was *Jimmy Ray!*"

"*What?*" Will sat up straight and scooted back in his seat. "He said I was with Jimmy Ray?"

"That's right." Carl leaned back and crossed his arms. "Ronny said that's how you introduced him."

Will's jaw hung low as he scanned the room like he was searching for words on the walls and ceiling. His eyes lit up as he snatched an idea out of thin air.

"That's not what I said," he finally blurted out. "The guy's name was *Jerry Grey*. Perez must have misunderstood."

"Really?" Carl glared from under his heavy brow. "You expect me to buy that? I don't know what you're worse at, betting or lying."

"Come on, Carl." Will threw his hands around in the air. "We were rolling around on the ground fighting over my gun. We were both pumped up on adrenaline. Maybe I slurred my words and he heard me wrong."

"Did Bam-Bam hear you wrong too?"

Will looked confused. "Bennett wasn't there."

"No, but I got the dump from Ronny's phone last night. Bennett called *and* texted right after you guys cornered him outside the bar. Bennett said he got a visit from Jimmy Ray and wanted to warn Ronny he might be next on the list."

"Well, there you go." Will slapped the table. "I had Jerry with me that night too. Bam-Bam's so damn paranoid he probably thought the guy was Jimmy Ray. After getting that call, Perez must have assumed the same thing. The names are close enough."

"Only one problem with that." Carl still stared like he was trying to burn a hole in his partner. "Bam-Bam was there when we busted Bernstein. He knows what Jimmy Ray looks like."

"You were there too," Will pointed out. "Could you pick him out of a line-up?"

"Bam-Bam saw him *inside* the coffee shop," Carl sneered. "I saw him in the alley. It was dark back there and you know it."

"It was also dark outside that bar when I questioned Bennett. Jerry has about the same build as the guy you caught. Maybe he looked enough like Jimmy Ray that Bam-Bam thought it was him."

"That's a load of shit, Doogie."

"Then maybe Jimmy Ray showed up after I left. We located Bennett without any trouble—Jimmy Ray could've found him too."

"That'd be one hell of a coincidence," Carl growled. "Jerry Grey, huh? You know I'm gonna look your guy up when we get to the office."

"Go ahead, but it's probably not his real name." Will had a crooked smile. "You just can't trust anybody these days."

Carl frowned and poked at his breakfast burrito. "I'm not turning loose of this Jimmy Ray thing until I find the bastard. You know that, right?"

Will held up his burrito and took a bite. "My money's on you, Jackrabbit."

Chapter 31

As soon as James and Missy entered the pub, Margie set her tray of dirty dishes down and made a beeline for the couple. She gave Missy a quick hug and then latched onto James, squeezing him extra tight.

"You had us all *so* worried, Jimmy!" As she relaxed her grip, the little woman reached up with one hand and smacked James on the back of the head. "Don't *ever* pull a stunt like that again, ya hear me?"

James held up his hands. "Loud and clear, Mom."

"Well, now it's official," Donny called out from behind the bar. "You're a full-fledged member of the Dugan Clan!"

"The initiation is just a head slap?" Missy laughed, dropped her purse on the bar, and mounted a stool. "I thought it was surviving the hangover you get from that stuff your mom keeps on the bottom shelf."

"Don't remind me." James made a face and took the seat next to her. "That bottle was responsible for my first hangover. Thank God for Miguel and his magic soup."

Missy cocked her head. "Magic soup?"

"Menudo," Donny replied, as he filled a couple of pint glasses for them. "He always keeps a bit stashed in the back of the fridge just in case."

"A life saver fer sure." Margie retrieved her tray and turned toward the kitchen. "Don't get too comfortable on those stools. We're sittin' down to a family dinner as soon as everybody gets here."

Missy grabbed her purse and stood up. "I guess that's my cue to leave."

Margie stopped and spun around. "Sit yerself back down there, girl. As long as yer with Jimmy, yer a part of this family, too." She winked at Missy. "Besides, if you up 'n leave now, me 'n Jen'll be outnumbered by the boys."

"Yes, ma'am!" Missy plopped back down and took a sip of her beer as Margie disappeared into the kitchen.

Donny leaned on the back counter. "Did you get your Rover towed outta the hills yet, Jimmy?"

"Deputy Yazzi helped me get it running yesterday. I was able to drive it home."

"How the hell did you manage that?" Donny raised a thick eyebrow. "I thought the battery was busted."

"I hate to admit it, but we did what Missy's uncle told me to do." James glanced sideways at his girlfriend. "We took the battery out, tied the positive cable up so it wouldn't short circuit, and then push-started it."

"Oh," Donny nodded. "You got a generator in that thing instead of an alternator, huh?"

James hung his head. "Am I the *only* one who didn't think of that?"

"It's not your fault." Missy patted him on the back. "You've never had to drive a piece of crap before."

"So, you finally admit that thing's a piece of crap. I told you that the first time I saw it." Will took the stool next to James and pointed at the bottom shelf. "Give me a double of the hard stuff, Donny. It's never a good thing when Mom rounds everybody up."

"Okay, but go easy." Donny snatched the bottle of amber liquid from its place and poured a small glass. "This stuff tends to put your mouth in high gear."

Missy rolled her eyes. "Yeah, like he needs help with *that*."

"Give me a break. It's been a hell of a day." Will took a drink and screwed his face up as he swallowed.

James sighed. "Did you get in trouble with Sergeant Miller because of me?"

"Are you kidding?" Will swirled the remaining whisky in his glass, then pushed it away. "Mike said with everything you've done, we should put you on the payroll."

"Really?" James perked up. "Maybe I could become a consultant."

"He was being sarcastic, Jimmy, but you did help get this case over with a little faster." Will scanned the room and lowered his voice. "If you hadn't played Jimmy Ray for me again, it would've taken a lot longer to get a name out of Bam-Bam—Perez, too. Mom doesn't know about that yet, does she?"

"No," James replied in a whisper. "And I think it would be safer for both of us if we kept it that way."

"You guys on board?" Will looked at Missy and Donny. "Not a word to Mom about the undercover stuff, okay?"

Missy gave a single nod. Donny winked and made a zipper motion across his lips.

"Good." Will turned his gaze back to James. "We might have one little problem. Perez said something to Carl about getting a visit from Willy-D and his boss."

"He knows you were with Jimmy Ray?" James took a deep breath and chugged half of his beer. Will caught his wrist and took the glass out of his hand.

"Slow down, Jimmy, I took care of it. I told him I was with a guy that has a similar name and the same build." Will set the glass down and put a hand on James' shoulder. "I don't think he totally bought it, but he's off the scent for now."

"What are we going to do? He's never giving this up, especially now that two people have actually seen my face recently. There's bound to be more talk on the streets."

"I'll tell you what we're gonna do." Will picked up his drink, swallowed the last mouthful, and grimaced. "We're putting Jimmy Ray out to pasture for good. Carl can't make the connection if there're no more sightings and no fresh trail to follow."

"But what if you need my help again?"

"Then I'll find another way," Will replied. "I'm not putting you in danger again. I might ask you for an opinion once in a while, maybe some help with research, but that's it. No more Jimmy Ray."

Missy tapped her nails on the bar. "Shut it, guys. Here comes your mom."

Will spun his stool around and came face to face with Margie. She wrapped her arms around him, gave him a kiss on the cheek and then stepped back.

"That's fer bringin' Jimmy home safe." She bunched up her fist and punched him in the shoulder. "An' *that's* fer getting' him mixed up in yer business again!"

Will rubbed his shoulder. "It's the last time, Mom. We talked it out and we're all good, right Jimmy?"

"Right." James held up his hands. "No more playing detective for me!"

"Alright then, everybody find a seat at the table." She motioned to Donny. "You too, son. Jen called an' she's almost here. Tell Robert to cover the bar for ya."

Margie headed into the back while the group made their way to the big table near the front of the pub. Unlike the rest of the tables with their woven baskets containing condiments and drink menus, this one was already set for a full meal. Stoneware plates edged with a delicate leaf pattern were flanked by cloth napkins and flatware several grades higher than the utensils normally found in the bar. James pulled a chair out for his girlfriend, then took the seat next to her. Will sat down across from them.

Missy squirmed in her chair. "So what's next for Ben and Uncle Walt?"

"Well, they've already been charged with growing and selling," Will replied. "That'll hold 'em until we finish the homicide investigation. Yazzi and I both witnessed Weber taking a shot at Jimmy, so he's also got an attempted murder charge too. Neither of those guys are going anywhere for a long time."

"Do you think I'll have to testify?" James asked.

"Depends on whether they take a plea or not. The evidence is piling up pretty deep. If the ballistics on those two guns come back positive, they'd be stupid to go to trial. With that many bodies, a jury would give them the death penalty for sure."

Missy scowled. "They both deserve it, but if it means Jimmy doesn't have to go to court, seeing them rotting in prison for the rest of their lives is fine with me."

James shook his head. "I still don't understand why they killed all those people."

"Money," Will replied. "With their product getting legalized all over the place, the demand on the street is shrinking. They were probably losing market-share, so they eliminated the competition."

"That's just sick." Missy frowned. "I still can't believe it was my own family."

"Speaking of family . . ." Will pointed over James' shoulder.

"Look who I found." Donny led his wife by the hand and sat her by Will, then took the seat next to her.

"I'm starvin'. Been smellin' that cabbage cookin' in the kitchen all day!"

Missy looked over at Jen. "Any idea what's going on? Your mother-in-law isn't saying anything."

"All in good time," she replied with a coy smile. "Actually, I'm surprised Donny hasn't spilled his guts yet."

"I know how to keep a secret." Donny grinned and winked at James.

When Margie rolled up to the table with a cart of food, James jumped up to help her unload the bounty. They set dishes down in the center of the table for a family style meal. Will immediately perked up.

"Is that lamb?"

He picked up his fork and reached toward the platter of braised meat. Jen elbowed him in the ribs as Margie reached over his shoulder and slapped his arm. Will quickly pulled his hand back.

"Not yet! We haven't said grace." Jen took the fork away and set it next to his plate. "You're worse than your brother."

"Quite a bit worse. Ya haven't been to church in years." Margie wrinkled her nose and took a seat next to James. "Jimmy, would you like to lead the blessing?"

"Umm . . ." James straightened up and put his hands in his lap. "I've never done it before. I don't even know how. I mean . . . my mom never . . ."

"It's okay, dear." Margie took one of his hands and squeezed it. "I shouldn't put ya on the spot like that. Donny, you do the honors."

James watched as everyone lowered their heads and made the sign of the cross. They moved their right hands from forehead to chest, then shoulder to shoulder. Missy poked him with her elbow and pointed. James caught on and mimicked the motions. As Donny spoke, everyone else joined in but James.

"Bless us, O Lord, and these, Thy gifts, which we are about to receive from Thy bounty. Through Christ, our Lord. Amen."

Everyone crossed themselves again—James followed suit before picking up his napkin and placing it on his lap.

Donny smiled as he passed a basket of bread around. "You're gonna need to learn that one, Jimmy. Next time she might twist yer arm."

James looked a little bewildered. "I've never prayed before."

Donny raised his eyebrows. "Never? Not even when you had a gun pointed at you?"

"It never entered my mind," James replied with a shrug. "My mom never talked about God. I think she stopped believing when my father died."

Jen glanced at Donny and then addressed James. "So what *do* you believe?"

James took a deep breath and scanned the faces around the table. Everyone had stopped eating and locked eyes on him. He began to flush. Small beads of sweat formed on his brow. It took a few moments for James to realize he had stopped breathing. He set his fork down and slowly exhaled.

"I . . . I don't know."

"I'm sorry. I probably shouldn't have asked." Jen looked at Margie and then at Donny again. "It's just that we—Donny and I—we have a question for you."

Margie nodded at Donny. "Go ahead an' ask him, son."

Donny sat up straight and cleared his throat. "Jimmy, I don't know how you feel about God, but I do know yer about the most moral person we know—no offense, Willy."

"None taken. The kid's got me beat big time in that department." Will smiled and filled his mouth with mashed potatoes.

"Okay, here goes." Donny took his wife's hand and continued. "Like I said, yer a moral and upstanding person . . . smart too."

Jen rolled her eyes. "Get to the point, Donny."

"The point is we're having this baby, see. What I'm saying is, we'd be honored if you'd be the child's godfather."

"Godfather?" James flushed again. "But I don't know the first thing about being a godfather."

Will grinned and wiped his mouth. "It's like in the movies, Jimmy. You get to have people wacked if they get outta line."

"Oh, shut up!" Jen let go of Donny's hand and smacked Will on the side of the head. "This is serious."

"Yes, it is." Margie turned to James. "As godfather, you'd be responsible fer givin' moral an' spiritual guidance to the child as he or she grows up."

"I'm touched and honored, but how am I supposed to give someone spiritual advice when I never received it myself?"

"Well, maybe it's time ya got some." Margie patted his hand. "Ya got a little time to figure it out."

James looked around the table. One by one, he gazed into the eyes of the group he now called his family. He felt his anxiety fade, replaced by a feeling of warmth.

"I can't tell you how much it means that you'd ask me." James swallowed a lump in his throat. "Just about a year ago, my mother passed away. I thought my life was over, but then I stumbled into this place."

"Actually, Mom *made* you come inside." Donny smirked. "You stumbled *out* after she got done with you!"

James laughed. "Yeah, I guess you're right, but something else happened that night too. I feel like maybe that's when I started living. Since that night, I've gained a real family—people who care about me."

James faced Donny and Jen. "My answer is . . . yes!"

Thank you for reading *Catching Karma*. If you enjoyed it, please take a moment to leave a review where you purchased my novel, and look for Killing Karma, the first James McCarthy adventure.

<u>About the Author</u>

I am an Arizona based writer of contemporary fiction. Using the Phoenix metropolitan area as a home base, my stories reflect the broad diversity of scenery and humanity found within The Grand Canyon State.

For information on upcoming books and projects, subscribe to my blog or follow me on Facebook.

Web: http://eldredbird.com
Facebook:
https://www.facebook.com/EldredBirdAuthor/

****

I would like to thank the following people, without whom this book could never have been completed.

Debi Bird – Chief Editor, Graphic Designer, and Understanding Wife
Ed & Joanne Robinson – Content and Line Editors
Donna Braunshausen – Final Proofreader
Laura T Emery – Friend, Fellow Author, and Critique Partner
The West Valley Writer's Critique Group of Avondale, Arizona – A special group of writers who took the time listen to me read every chapter out loud, and then told me what I *needed* to hear, not what I *wanted* to hear.

Made in the USA
San Bernardino, CA
28 March 2017